MW01038565

The Newtonian Egg

AND OTHER CASES OF ROLF LE ROUX

The Newtonian Egg

AND OTHER CASES OF ROLF LE ROUX

PETER GODFREY

Crippen & Landru Publishers
Norfolk, Virginia
2002

FIRST EDITION
1 2 3 4 5 6 7 8 9 10

Crippen & Landru Publishers, Inc.
P. O. Box 9315
Norfolk, VA 23505
USA

www.crippenlandru.com
CrippenL@Pilot.Infi.net

To Rose Dannay
in memory of the great man (alas! no longer with us) who was her
beloved husband and my friend and mentor

—Peter Godfrey

CONTENTS

PETER GODFREY

Peter Godfrey, my father, brought the fictional "Oom" (Uncle) Rolf le Roux into our family in the 1950s. The strange, brilliant, bearded fellow who analysed the world, squinting through hanging scarves of pipesmoke was ubiquitous — not only in our house in Johannesburg, South Africa (where he was a subject of much discussion) but also in the Golden City itself where in short story guise he stalked book shops; and popped up in theatres where his exploits were staged and applauded.

But clean–shaven Dad who by his own description was "6 ft 2 inches in all directions" resembled his creation only in some ways. Like Oom Rolf, he was sensitive, as aware of human motivation as any scene–of–crime psychologist. Above all, like his story character, he was fascinated by criminology. But Peter, a man whose complexity and versatility constantly surprised even his own family, was certainly less dour than Oom. True, Oom loved poetry but you couldn't imagine that mature, steady–eyed fact–dismantler ever removing his pipestem long enough to quote, let alone write the giggleworthy: "The Leopard is peppered, and peppered with spots. She's got lots. Now the jaguar and cheetah, *believe* they can beetah, but spot–wise they're not wise. They're clots!"

On the other hand the intricacy of Dad's cartoon–poetry would have pleased Oom who would have deduced from it that its author was a man who hitched a powerful sense of orderliness to verbal brevity. He would have concluded: "Undoubtedly an experienced journalist and the sort of fiction writer who is convinced that with the solidity of plot in place the words should look after themselves." As usual, Oom Rolf's assessment would have been right.

Peter Godfrey was born in 1917 in Vereeniging, Transvaal — a place then famous as the spot on which the Anglo–Boer peace treaty was signed and later notorious as the town which possessed a "Native Township" called Sharpeville where 63 black residents were massacred by the white police in 1960.

9

Educated at school and university in Johannesburg he carved for himself a varied and fruitful career in journalism, at times being a crime expert, a columnist, a parliamentary correspondent, court reporter, editor of a popular magazine and, ultimately in South Africa, editor of the famous African magazine, *Drum*, reflecting his loathing of, and dangerously public opposition to, apartheid.

In the interim, he became a well–known radio commentator on unsolved mysteries. He was also responsible for the material on a top–ranking quiz programme and devised cryptic crosswords and various other types of puzzles for South African periodicals (cue for a wry smile from Mr Le Roux).

He came to London in 1962, joined later by my mother, Nina, my elder brother, Dennis and me. There, he continued his journalistic career on *The Daily Herald*, *The Sun* and was well–established on *the London Times* when he retired.

But his life as writer of fiction was entirely separate. He wrote his first short story on the night the A–bomb fell on Hiroshima. Eventually he was to write hundreds, many of which were to win awards, particularly in the USA, for short detective fiction. He also wrote for stage, television and radio. One of his longer tales was made into the United Artists film, *The Girl in Black Stockings*, starring Ann Bancroft.

In one of his more lucid moments before his death in the London Hospital in 1992 he asked us to warn the nurses not to serve him Newtonian eggs before breakfast. Oom Rolf, nodding, pipe in hand, would have concurred.

—Ronald Godfrey

AUTHOR'S PREFACE

Shortly after World War II — the latter end of the period dubbed by critics the Golden Age of detective fiction — Peter Godfrey, then living in South Africa, was producing a stream of short stories, which appeared in top magazines all over the world.

His most popular creation was the homicide squad of the Cape Town C.I.D., which was featured as a series in the prestigious *Ellery Queen's Mystery Magazine*, won several awards, and is still frequently reprinted in present day anthologies.

Titular head of the homicide team was Lieutenant Dirk Joubert, aggressive and painstaking. He was assisted by Johnson, a young and eager Detective Sergeant. Third and most important was Rolf le Roux, a lawyer with a degree in abnormal psychology, kindly, humane and deeply perceptive, a special adviser to lieutenant Joubert. He was not a policeman, but had been seconded by the Public Prosecutor's office after a series of court debacles involving the Cape Town homicide team.

It should be remembered that in the period covered by these stories, right up to the present day, murder is a capital crime in South Africa. Convicted murderers are invariably hanged, except where grounds for clemency exist, when the statutory death sentence is commuted to life imprisonment.

THE NEWTONIAN EGG

The story which follows received a special Ellery Queen award in 1951 as an "unclassifiable" story. Ellery Queen himself explained why in an introductory note. He said: "It cannot be fully described as a whodunit, a whydunit or a howdunit – for the simple reason that the tale has in it the solid elements of all three 'tec types. It is also an impossible–crime story, or to put it another way, a miracle problem. Similarly, it can be designated a sealed–room story – in this instance a sealed egg; and from a completely different point of view it can be labelled a broken alibi story. Read it, and decide for yourself."

"The dying man," said Hal Brooke, "ate a hearty wedding breakfast."

On the other side of the room Kurtz, also with a tray on his knees, sneered. He said: "It's a funny thing about this disease, you can feel on top of the world one minute, and knocking at the pearly gates the next. Even if you are getting married this afternoon, you could pop off just as well today as any other day." He grinned. "Maybe the excitement will make it even more likely. You know, I've been thinking about it for the last few minutes — trying to imagine which would be the most appropriate moment for you to kick the bucket. At first I thought during the cere-mony... but there's a better time."

"Yes?"

"Yes. In that fraction of a second before the final consum-mation. Although, of course, any time today would still be poeti-cally satisfying."

Brooke said softly: "You love me very much, don't you, Kurtzie?"

In the third bed, Winton moved his bandaged wrists, moaned and cursed. "Shut up!" he said. "Shut up! We've got to die — we know that. But why keep talking about it? Why talk?"

"Winton," said Kurtz "doesn't like talk. Oh no. He prefers action — only he bungles his actions. When you managed to steal that scalpel, Winton, why didn't you just cut your throat and have done with it? Didn't you realise the nurses would be bound to discover your cut wrists before anything serious happened? Or did you just go through the motions, with some half–witted idea of gaining sympathy?"

"I should've used it on you," said Winton. "It would've stopped your infernal talking."

"Minds," said Brooke. "Funny things. Look at yours, Kurtz. A good brain, education and experience behind it, a capacity to think constructively when you choose. Only, you don't choose. You prefer to twist and distort into the meanest, most personal, ugliest channels you can conceive. A real mental prostitution. And then there's you, Winton — no real mind at all, only a few cockeyed emotions. No intelligence. Just a sort of blind stretching forward to satisfy the need of the moment."

Winton said: "What do you know about what goes on in my mind? What about the scalpel? Could you have got one, Mr. Genius?"

"If I wanted one," said Brooke, "I'd get one. And if I wanted to use it, I'd use it properly. I don't know how you got it, Winton, but I'm pretty certain it was by accident. And I'm not running down your lack of mind through malice. Oh no. You're the luckiest of the three of us. When you go, you've got so very little to lose."

Winton cursed. He repeated: "How do you know what I think about?"

"I don't — except by inference. But let's find out. Take this boiled egg for instance. Here, let me hold it in my hand. Now, look at it, and tell me what you think."

As Winton hesitated, Kurtz laughed from his bed. "Come on, Winton, I want to hear this, too."

"It's just... an egg," said Winton. "Laid by a hen, on a farm somewhere. And boiled here in the kitchen."

"And brought to me, warm, white and unbroken," said Brooke. "I know. That's how your mind works. But this egg tells my mind a lot more."

"Like what?"

"Oh, many things... It reminds me, for instance, of Isaac Newton, of his discoveries — the law of gravitation — and from there, of space and time and the universe, of Einstein and relativity. And it reminds me on the other side, of pre–Newton science, of the theories of the transmutation of metals; and I see that Newton is the link, and the two sides of the chain meet again today in the atom physicists."

"You're talking nonsense," said Winton. "What has an egg to do with Isaac Newton?"

"Ah, so you haven't even heard that story? Let me tell it to you — maybe it will provide some consolation for you. It shows how even great minds have their moments of aberration... You see, a friend once came into Newton's kitchen, and there was the savant holding an egg in the palm of his hand — like this — staring at it in utter concentration — and on the stove next to him his watch boiled merrily in a pot of water."

Again, Kurtz laughed. Winton looked at Brooke uncertainly. He said: "You're still talking in the air... "

But Brooke was warming to his theme. "The human mind," he said, "What a magnificent mechanism! Properly applied, it creates miracles. Nothing, basically is impossible — "

"Except us." In his triumph Winton spat. "What about us? All the best brains in science, all working on us, and they can't help. None of them can help."

Kurtz said: "All the same, Brooke's right. One day they'll find a cure. Maybe the day after you die, Winton. Or the day before. That's why your scalpel idea was so completely and utterly foolish."

"They still need data," said Brooke. "Sorry, I should have been more explicit. I should have said nothing is basically impossible when all the facts are known. Do you ever read detective stories?"

Winton said: "Trash."

"Not all of them. I'm thinking of a particular story, written by a man who's now dead — Jacques Futrelle. A magnificent story called 'The Problem of Cell 13.' Futrelle's hero is a man he calls The Thinking Machine. He claimed that if he were locked in the condemned cell under the usual conditions, with nothing except his own magnificent mental equipment, he would think himself out. And he did, Winton, he did."

"In a story, yes. Anything's possible in a story."

"Logic is the common denominator between good fiction and life. That's why I say your scalpel idea was clumsy. There are so many easier, more ingenious methods. Now, if I wanted to get rid of myself — ”

"No," said Kurtz. "I don't like suicide — not even used as an example. Rather, assume that you were planning to kill Winton. Or better still, that I wanted to kill you. Much truer to life."

"All right, we'll say you want to kill me. And that you use your mind in the way that you ought to use it. You'll pick something commonplace and apparently innocent, like — like this egg here. Yes, the egg's a good idea. First you lay your hands on some virulent poison — if Winton could find a scalpel, you most certainly could find some poison. And you would work out a method of getting the poison inside the unbroken shell of the egg — ”

Winton said: "That's an impossibility, Brooke, a complete impossibility."

"Is it? That's what they said about The Thinking Machine and his guarded cell. And there's another angle, too — also from detective fiction. In a book called *The Three Coffins* one of the modern masters of detective fiction, John Dickson Carr, had his chief character give a lecture on how to commit murder in a hermetically sealed room. If I remember correctly, there were three main methods, each with dozens of variations. And all perfectly possible — remember that, Winton. And if a murderer can get into a sealed room, commit a murder and disappear, he could also get into a sealed egg. The same principles apply. And the egg could be brought to me like this one, through the normal innocent channels, and I could crack the shell, as I'm doing now, scoop up the egg — yes, do all the natural things, absolutely unsuspecting, put the spoon in my mouth, and die."

He put the spoonful of egg into his mouth.

And died.

❂

"Mr. le Roux," said nurse Metter, and then: "No, I can't call you that. Hal has told me so much about you. I'm going to call you Rolf, and you must call be Doris. I can't go on calling my husband's best friend by his surname, can I?"

"Definitely not." The brown eyes twinkled, and behind the beard the full lips curved into a smile. "I would like to have come earlier, but Hal's letter didn't give me much time. Still, I suppose I'll have a chance for a chat with him before the ceremony?"

"Of course. The padre won't get here until after lunch, and you can see Hal as soon as he's finished his breakfast. He's in Ward 3 just down the passage. You can follow me in when I go to fetch the trays. They'll be ringing for me any second now."

Rolf remembered the letter from Hal in his pocket. And he thought: "Nice girl. If only Hal could live his normal span... "

The girl must have seen something of his mental images. "I'm afraid I'm just a little bit nervous," she said. "You see, it's not every day — "

She turned as the buzzer behind her sounded, and Rolf noticed that the numeral "3" had dropped in the indicator. But the buzzer kept on, urgently, persistently.

"Oh," said Doris Metter. "Something's wrong!"

She whirled past Rolf, moved in long–limbed strides down the passage. He came after her. Just inside the door of Ward 3 she paused momentarily, clutching her throat with one hand.

The contorted body of Hal Brooke sprawled in a half–sitting position on the bed, knees drawn up and twisted as though from a violent spasm. There was a thin line of froth on his lips.

Doris Metter said "Oh" again, ran forward, stumbled over the tray and crockery on the floor, struggled back to her feet, threw herself sobbing on the breast of the corpse on the bed.

Rolf le Roux said to the man in the bed opposite: "Keep ringing the bell." He put his hands on Doris Metter's shoulders and gently drew her away. While doing so, he caught the elusive smell, bent over the body to make certain. When he straightened again, his face was very grave.

Another nurse came to the door of the Ward, hesitated only long enough to call out down the passage, and hurried forward. She caught the sobbing figure of Doris Metter in her arms, and started to lead her gently from the room. They were only halfway to the door when the young doctor came in, took in the significance of the scene, went to the living before the dead. He spoke quickly, consolingly; gave crisp instructions to the other nurses. Only then he came to look at the body.

He said to Rolf: "You're Mr. le Roux, of course, Hal told me all about you. I'm Randall." And then: "This must have been a bad shock for you. Tragic, under the circumstances. But you must remember it could be expected to happen at any time."

Rolf's eyes were hard and implacable. "Smell his lips," he said.

Randall looked at him for a long second, then bent over the body. His expression changed. He said: "I see."

The man in the bed opposite shook his head, as though to clear it. "Poison," he said conversationally. "And it was suicide, you know, even though it probably doesn't look like it. Brooke was talking about suicide just before it happened."

The third patient sat up in bed, waved a bandaged wrist. "You're a liar, Kurtz. He was talking about you killing him."

"Here," said Randall suspiciously, "what's all this?"

"I'll tell you," said Kurtz. "I think I remember almost every word of the conversation. And don't interrupt until I've finished, Winton. You can say all you want to, then." Rapidly he sketched out the conversation. "Is that right?"

"That's right," said Winton grudgingly.

Dr. Randall grimly got down on hands and knees, sniffed over the shattered egg that was lying on the floor, looked up, and nodded.

"And the egg," said Rolf, "was opened by Brooke? Is that all that happened?"

"That's all," said Winton.

Randall started to say: "There's no way of getting potassium cyanide into an unbroken — " He stopped, because Kurtz was shaking with laughter.

"Poor old Winton and his literal mind," said Kurtz. "How Brooke would have loved to hear him now! Of course something else happened, but something so casual and commonplace that Winton would never think of mentioning it."

"And that was?"

"Brooke cracked the egg, and took the spoonful to his mouth, and he was talking all the time. But between these two actions he did something else. He took the salt–cellar from the cruet, poured a quantity on the surface of the egg, and mixed it in with the spoon. And only then did he take his mouthful."

"You mean," asked Randall, "the salt — ?" But while he was still speaking, Rolf was already on the floor, searching among the debris of the fallen tray.

"There it is," said Winton, "still lying on the bed."

Randall picked it up off the counterpane, unscrewed the top, and held the body of the container to his nose. He took one of the white grains, smelled it again to make sure, and touched it with his tongue. "No," he said, "this is ordinary table salt."

"So," said Kurtz, and looked quizzically at Rolf le Roux.

But Rolf said, almost to himself, "The timing... " and then, "How long did it take? I mean everything — from the moment the nurse left the breakfast trays to the moment she came back in answer to your ring?"

"Four or five minutes," said Kurtz.

"No," said Winton. "Longer than that. Say eight or nine."

"And all the time you both stayed in bed? You did not move?"

"I stayed in bed," said Winton. "But I don't know about Kurtz. I was too busy looking at Brooke to notice what Kurtz did."

Kurtz smiled. "I stayed in bed, too." He looked at Rolf. "You know, Brooke was a real admirer of yours. He advertised you — the great Sherlock of the Cape Town C.I.D. It's rather interesting to watch you now — standing there, baffled over Newton's egg."

"Not Newton's egg," said Rolf. "Newton's apple."

❂

Except for the corpse, he was alone in the Ward. Kurtz and Winton had been searched and taken out. Dr. Randall had gone down the passage to telephone the police post at Bossiesfontein.

He pulled the letter out of his pocket and read it again.

Dear Rolf,

If you ask me how I am, I will tell you that I am dying very nicely, thank you. Which is in direct contrast to the other two unfortunates in this ward. We all three are under sentence of death with intestinal T.B.; but, speaking strictly for myself, once you get accustomed to the feeling of general malaise and the knowledge that any given morning — if you will forgive the Irishism — you may wake up to find yourself dead, you can find some compensations, even in the valley of the shadow.

In my own case, I am delighted to find that my wits have never been so sharp and crystal–clear and — now hold on to your malodorous pipe! — I am also getting married.

Don't get a shock — it's all perfectly feasible and natural. I've checked with the quacks here, and read up all the authorities myself just to make sure, and this is certain — the disease, in the form I have it, is neither contagious nor infectious, nor transmissible by heredity. And think of this, Rolf — I can still partially cheat death if I have a child.

And I am going to have that child. It's all arranged. One of the doctors here by the name of Randall pulled strings — particularly decent of him because I think he's got a soft spot for Doris himself. (Oh, yes, of course, I should have told you — the girl is a nurse here, Doris Metter.) Anyway, he's doing everything possible. After the ceremony we move straight into a private Ward. Doris has been examined, too, and is 100% healthy.

I know this all sounds like cold–blooded stud arrangements, but I may not have the time to waste on tact and social graces. I want a child, and I want a healthy child — one that has a chance to make better use of its life than I have.

Doris not only understands, she shares my urge. Last night she told me why. You see, she had an elder brother she worshipped, and he also died of an incurable disease — haemophilia — at the age of 14. I suppose there is basically some sort of Freudian identification in her mind between me and her brother, and she feels that in our child — and it'll be a son for sure — she'll have me and her brother too. But that's not entirely the whole story for either of us. You see, old–timer, we're really in love.

The ceremony is on Tuesday — and don't you dare send me your congratulations by letter. I want to hear them verbally, direct from the labyrinths of your beard. If you catch a train from Cape Town on Sunday night, you should be here on the morning of the marriage, the lucky day.

More when I see you in the flesh —
   Hal.

Not the letter of a suicide, thought Rolf. And yet, in three days much could happen. The half–life he was living, the twisted motives...

To decide definitely, there were many other things to be found out. Access to poisons, for instance. Opportunity, generally. More facts were needed, new angles. Sometimes, looked at from a different direction, the impossible became obvious... and he owed it to Hal to make absolutely sure.

❁

Rolf found Dr. Randall sitting at the desk in the office along the passage. He asked, "Have you contacted the police?"

"No," said Randall. "I was... well, to tell the truth, I was waiting for you. I wanted to have a talk."

"Yes?"

"I... Look here, must I call the police? Won't you forget about the poison — let me sign the death certificate? What good will it do with the police prying around, badgering Dor— Nurse Metter? What for? Isn't it enough that Hal's dead, without him also being branded a suicide? Isn't it really better my way?"

Rolf said: "Maybe it would be... easier. But what if it was not suicide? Would you want his murderer to go scot–free?"

Randall was deeply upset. "Don't forget, he was a doomed man in any case. And who could have killed him? Kurtz? Winton? Also doomed men. Is it worthwhile putting all this further torture on an innocent girl?"

"Hal Brooke was my friend," said Rolf. He sat for a moment, with his eyes far away. "For his sake, and if I were sure... but I first have to be sure, you understand. We can wait two hours, and after that I promise you I will make up my mind."

"Thank you, Mr. le Roux. And if I can help in any way — ?"

"First, I'd like to know where the poison could have come from."

"In all probability from this room. From that closet over there."

"Locked?"

"Well, yes — but actually the lock slips if you give a sharp jerk on the door. We should have had it repaired, of course, only... well, it's just been neglected."

Rolf was staring at the serried bottles and jars on the shelf. He located the tiny potassium cyanide container, and scratched his beard contemplatively. He said: "One thing I don't understand... there are poisons here, yes, but there are also harmless drugs. Isn't it unusual to keep them together?"

"Not if you realise that, being so far from town, we dispense most of our own medicines, and that this room is our dispensary."

"Even so, isn't potassium cyanide rather a strange drug to have here?"

"No, it's a common drug in a T.B. hospital. It's used in making up a very effective cough mixture. A tiny quantity, of course — the basis is a minim two drops to eight ounces of other ingredients."

"I see. And so it is perfectly possible for one of the patients to walk in here, if he knows about the room, jerk open the locked cupboard, and remove a quantity of poison? Could this be done unseen?"

"Definitely. It was from this room, we think, that Winton stole the scalpel with which he tried to commit suicide. But it would have to be done late at night. During the day, if I am not here, there's a nurse on duty."

"Have you actually noticed that anything here was interfered with at any time?"

"No. I can honestly say I've seen nothing."

"But?"

"Well, when I came and sat down here just now, I had a feeling that there was something wrong, something somehow out of place. Just a vague feeling... "

❂

She lay on the bed in the darkened room, and if she had been weeping the atmosphere of the tragedy would have seemed less.

"There's nothing to talk about," she said. "It's just... horrible. And I don't think you would understand."

"Perhaps I would," said Rolf. "He was my friend, you know. And he wrote me all about the situation. Let me talk, rather. You can tell me whether I am right... You see, I know what he wanted — how he felt about having a child. And how you felt. And it seems to me that, even though you loved him, the horror is not so much Hal dying. You knew it would happen, and you were prepared for it. No, the horror in your mind is that the child will never be born, that Hal will not live again in your child, that you have nothing of him left... "

She started to cry — hoarse, racking sobs. "Yes," she said, "yes." And then: "I couldn't even give him his last wish." She heaved convulsively in her sobbing. "I had a brother once — " and then gave herself over to a paroxysm of grief. After a while she quieted. "He wanted a child so badly. That's the irony of it. So badly that... and his face, when he heard from Dr. Randall that I had been examined, that there was nothing wrong with me, that I could have his son, a healthy son... That was all that he had left in life, Rolf."

He waited for her, then he asked: "When you brought him his tray in the morning, was there anything about it that was different?"

"No," she said. It was his usual breakfast. A soft–boiled egg and coffee."

"And the others in the ward — did they also have boiled eggs?"

"No. Kurtz's egg was fried, and Winton had an omelette."

"Was Hal's egg in any way cracked?"

"No. It was just an egg. I gave the order in the kitchen, and a few minutes later took the three trays in."

"And after that?"

"I had more trays to carry to other Wards. And then I heard that you were here, and I came to speak to you. You know... the rest."

"Yes. But tell me this — from the time you took Hal his tray to the moment we went back to the Ward, how long do you think it was?"

"A long time," she said. At least twenty–five minutes."

❋

Rolf le Roux came back to the dispensary, sat down at the desk, and put his head in his hands. Motive, he thought, that was the key... the motive for suicide — or murder. And he thought again of that last conversation in the Ward, the dying man's lecture on Jacques Futrelle and John Dickson Carr. A sealed egg, yes, and Isaac Newton... looking at the egg while the watch boiled... the law of gravitation...

Because his thoughts were travelling in circles he opened his eyes, emptied his mind and looked around the room.

And looking, he felt what the doctor had experienced before him, the vague unease that a pattern was wrong, that something was out of position. And right in front of his eyes, on the bookshelf above the desk he saw what it was:

The huge volumes of the *British Encyclopaedia of Medical Practice*. Volumes 1,2,3,4,5,7,6,8 — volumes 7,6. One out of place. Which?

The index of volume 7 told him nothing. He turned to volume 6. Gout, granuloma, haemophilia, haem — Haemophilia. He remembered Hal's letter.

Page 123, Definition: An hereditary disease, only affecting males. Prognosis: Grave. A fatal illness, and generally fatal in childhood. Females cannot have it, but they do transmit it to male offspring. And Doris' brother died of haemophilia. That meant the disease had been transmitted through her mother. And if Doris herself had a male child it would... No, that wasn't quite right. Her male child might have haemophilia. Not would.

I know something about genetics, thought Rolf, and yet I very nearly made that mistake. A layman reading first paragraphs and then skipping over the formulae beneath would almost certainly fall into the mental trap, be sure that if Doris bore a boy it would certainly be a haemophiliac.

Here was a motive. Yes, for suicide. If Hal, with his searching curiosity had crept in here last night, had looked at the book — and someone had obviously looked at the book — how would he have reacted? The poison closet so handy... but where would he keep it? What would he use as a container? Would he, with his tidy mind, have destroyed himself without warning Doris of the peril of her blood?

And besides, it was a motive for murder too. Randall, in love with Doris, fond of Hal... Suppose he only heard last night that her brother had died of the disease. Suppose he came here to check the truth, and he knew about Hal's urge for the child and Doris'... Might he not have resolved to kill to save her future misery? He had been anxious enough to sign a death certificate... No. Not a doctor. Such reasoning would be incredible for a doctor.

Could it be something else, something apart from this, some motive pointing the finger at Kurtz or Winton?

The truth...

He saw it. And the room whirled.

Isaac Newton, he thought. How it all came back to him. The talk about the egg... and then the proof that Kurtz had actually named the murder weapon. The saltcellar. Because if a man took salt from a cruet stand, when finished he would most likely replace the cellar in the cruet. Especially if he were eating off the limited surface of a tray. Or he would put it on the tray. And his death in paroxysms, if the cruet, the tray, everything fell to the floor, then the saltcellar would also fall. Like Newton's apple, obeying the laws of gravitation. And if the saltcellar were found on the bed, then someone must have put it there. Or rather, put an innocent saltcellar on the bed —

After gaining possession of the poisoned one.

And then there was the final irrefutable psychological proof: the perception of time.

Newton and his egg again. A subtlety — the great man's mind was wandering into absent-minded reverie, because although he was staring at what he thought was his watch, he wasn't really seeing it. His mind was wandering because if he concentrated on his watch the egg would seem to take longer to boil.

Kurtz said four or five minutes; Winton said eight or nine. But Doris Metter thought it was twenty-five minutes. Because she had been waiting for it to happen.

And Rolf saw her again, in the cold light of his mind, stumble over the tray on the floor, rise to her feet, weep on the breast of the corpse. And the action formed two clear patterns. Picking up the poisoned saltcellar, putting down the innocent one.

But he saw also another image. He saw her, last night, the night before her wedding day, standing in the dispensary, picking up the medical book on a curious impulse, reading, and having her whole world collapse in a few lines. And he saw into her mind, too, into the torment and chaos, crystallising in the soul–tearing illogic of her resolution. In his ears again he heard her voice, bubbling through her tears: "I couldn't even give him his last wish, Rolf — not even his last wish."

Rolf le Roux stood up, slowly and heavily and he walked along the corridor until he met Dr. Randall, and he said: "I have made a mistake. You may sign the death certificate."

THE FIFTH DIMENSION

Cape Town, March 16, 1960

My Dear Lieutenant Joubert,

By the time you get this letter you will no doubt know all about me — or else I have underrated my old friends at Scotland Yard for the second time in my career. If they have not made contact with you already I can assure you they will reply exceedingly promptly to any query you may make. And among other things they will impress on you that I am most emphatically a man of my word.

I stress this latter point because, in my first attempt to test the intelligence of the South African police, I am about to make you a promise. But I will come to that later.

First, let me tell you about the marvellous little gadget I have completed. Ever since I reached Cape Town three and a half weeks ago, I have been working on it night and day, and I am very happy to report that it has passed all its tests. I have referred to the mechanism as a "gadget," because I feel the description "infernal machine" is rather too pedantic to use between friends.

But I am digressing — a bad habit of mine which I hope you will learn to pardon.

This gadget of mine would never be taken for what it really is without the closest inspection — it resembles in every charac-teristic something so commonplace and innocent that it would never be suspected — and I intend to put it to practical use in the very near future.

Four people were killed on the last occasion I made a similar gadget, and I am hoping to improve considerably on those figures on the present occasion. The mechanism now controls an explosive force at least six times as powerful as previously. On the last occasion, the British press, in the absence of any direct evidence as to what caused the explosion, referred to a "bomb outrage." On this

27

occasion I hope your journalists will use their imagination. A single bomb would be an inept description of the improved gadget. I would be most disappointed if they do not refer to the cause as a "stick of bombs."

You will be hearing from me with further details shortly. That is my promise.

Yours sincerely,

Tom Lereto

✪

Cable from Chief Inspector Brentwood to Lieutenant Joubert:

New Scotland Yard, March 16, 1960

Re: your query Lereto. This man is dangerous. Escaped January 17 from Broadmoor Asylum for the criminally insane, had no idea he had left England or would have warned you previously. Intensive search for him was being prosecuted here.

Lereto is aged 46, thin, slight, with dark greying hair and brown eyes. Inconspicuous and appears rational. Fingerprint classification: I/I U/U oo/oo 10/30. Photos are being radioed. Hold Lereto for extradition.

Record: Responsible for bomb explosion in Bristol post office January 1957. Four dead. Responsible for release of poison gas in London subway March 1958. No fatalities but 32 hospital cases. Arrested while attempting to poison Dorking water supply April 1959. Committed to Broadmoor June 4 1959. Escaped January 17 1960.

Modus Operandi: Has delusion that his mission is to test the efficiency of the police force. Sends warning letters to the C.I.D. chief in the district where he contemplates outrage. Take any such letter seriously. Allusions in his Dorking letter caused his arrest. Medical opinion at Broadmoor is that Lereto will never commit offence without first sending warning.

Further details: Lereto is first–class mechanic, clock–maker, wood–worker, chemist, amateur actor. It is believed, but there is no proof, that he stays in the vicinity of the outrage to observe effects. Please report developments urgent.

❁

Cape Town, March 17, 1960
My dear Inspector Joubert,

Are you surprised at hearing again from me so soon? To be quite frank with you, I am so fascinated with the idea of the explosion I am organising, that it would try my patience far too much to delay matters. Admittedly, I am giving you very little time, but I am compensating for that in other directions, as you will soon see. In any event if you have not already cabled Scotland Yard for their opinion as to my sincerity, you will be able to do so today.

Zero hour is 11 a.m. tomorrow. Or rather, to be more accurate, at 11 a.m. sharp I will depress a trigger — a small spring — in my latest invention. The explosion will occur between four and seven minutes after that time. I am sorry I cannot be more accurate; you will, of course, appreciate that the gadget is a prototype — after gaining more experience, I hope to let you have the exact second of explosion in all my future models.

But again I am wandering from the point. I promised you more details; let me keep my promise.

Firstly, the place. I have chosen a large public building in the central area of Cape Town. I am afraid I cannot be more specific. Remember, I am testing your intelligence, and to go into more details would rather defeat that purpose. I have no desire to feed you with information to the extent that you are waiting for me when I arrive. But even though there are several public buildings, I contend, that by a process of elimination by mentally associating yourself with me, you should be able to deduce which one. Take my advice then, Lieutenant — do not give way to panic. Choose your most com— fortable chair to sit on, and concentrate hard. If you are patient enough, the solution will come to you eventually.

Secondly — but you already know everything. You know who will be responsible, the motives, the method, the time, the place. You know the four W's that journalists contend is necessary to cover all aspects of a report. You know Who, Why, Where, and When. Or, in the language of measurement, you know the height, the breadth, the depth, and the space–time of the problem. And that is what fascinates me. With all these details you still do not know enough to prevent the experiment. For that you still need another W — a fifth dimension.

Yes, that is what this experiment has, and what you must find if you are to prevent it. A fifth dimension... it sounds impossible, an impractical metaphysical abstraction, and yet it is true. Not only true, but a very simple truth, a self–evident truth. Maybe, in formulating this plan I have hit on an illustration — a very simple illustration — of a great truth which may one day be expressed in a complicated mathematical formula by a new Einstein.

But all that, of course, belongs to the remote future. You and I need only concern ourselves with the present — the hours from now until 11 a.m. tomorrow.

Need I stress that I will be watching your reaction with great interest?

Yours sincerely,

Tom Lereto.

❄

The place was Caledon Square.
The date March 17, 1960.

In the early hours of the morning there was a long conference in Inspector Joubert's office, and for a long time there seemed to be an abnormal number of thick–set men in plain clothes coming to and leaving the building. But from the time the city awoke, there was nothing in the conduct of police headquarters to indicate anything different from normal police routine.

The tension was all confined to the four walls of Joubert's office, and it did not seep through to permeate the routine. Rather, it was the routine that edged into the room...

In the charge office facing Buitenkant Street, Sergeant Koggel was on duty, and the normal number of uniformed men was in evidence. The good sergeant looked out of the window at the overcast sky, and waited patiently for the inevitable Saturday morning procession of friends and relatives coming to release the Friday night drunks. He paged through the occurrences book, and noted that all the drunks were named Smith, Jones or Brown. That was an advantage — it meant that they were all old hands, either their friends would come to pay their admission of guilt without comment, or else they would be transported in bulk to the Magistrate's Court. In any event, they would be dealt with swiftly, and that was all to the good. On this morning Koggel had special instructions. He was to provide the facade, the appearance of normality. No-one should be able to guess from the appearance of the charge office that the C.I.D. rooms were empty, their occupants scattered since early morning, all looking for a little Englishman who wasn't right in the head.

Of course, if a drastic necessity arose, then Inspector Joubert... but Koggel did not want that necessity to arise. He had been given additional responsibility; he was on his mettle. The time was then 8.35 and he braced himself conscientiously as an attorney, whom he knew well, came to release the first drunk.

Upstairs, and even behind the closed door of Joubert's room, the silence in the other offices could be felt.

On the surface Joubert looked as dapper as ever; only those who knew him well would have been able to detect the signs of lack of sleep and strain. Both the other men in the office showed the same symptoms. Detective–Sergeant Johnson's cheeks were not as ruddy as usual and his usually–clear eyes were red. Rolf le Roux, gripped the stem of his pipe behind his beard, but for once he was making no attempt to smoke it. He was poring over a docket which contained two letters and a cablegram.

"I don't think we've left anything undone," said Joubert, "but just in case, let's tick off the points as they occur. First, even if we wanted to, we could not cover every public building in Cape Town, but in view of the information from the British police, I think we are quite justified in taking Lereto's letter literally, and concentrating only on those public buildings in the central area of the city."

He looked at the others for confirmation. Both nodded.

"Right. Then as far as city buildings are concerned, we can eliminate several major headaches — the railway police are taking care of Railways and Harbours property. That leaves us the House of Assembly, the Senate, the various government offices, the Post Office, the Library, the South African Museum, the Art Gallery, the Magistrate's Courts, the Revenue Office, the Provincial Admini-stration Buildings, the Supreme Court, the City Hall, the Cape Archives, the Michaelis Art Gallery, the Koopmans de Wet House and the Martin Melck House. Oh, yes, and of course, the Castle — but the military are in control there, and don't need us. Anything I've left out?"

Johnson said, "You know there are several other buildings which might be called 'public'. What about the Technical College? And the various banks?"

"Well, we've got to take a chance on them — although they will be partly covered by the squad we've got on the Round City beat. At 11.00 there'll be at least one man covering each of these places. All the same, I've got the feeling that when Lereto used the word 'public' he was using it in the sense of 'publicly owned.' What do you think, Oom?"

Rolf said, "I think you are right, and for that reason can exclude the banks. On the other hand, the Technical College is publicly owned. It is hardly likely Lereto will choose that building — his letters seem to indicate a place of more general importance — but can you afford to take that chance?"

"No," said Joubert, and then "Johnson, when you go out at 10.30, pull the men off the banks and concentrate them as a squad to guard the Tech. Same principle as the other squads. Watch out for suspicious characters, clear the building completely just before 11.00, and allow nobody to come near until at least 11.30."

"Or until I hear an explosion from another part of town." But this time Johnson was not being facetious.

✪

Downstairs, Sergeant Koggel had reached his first crisis of the morning. He explained for the fifth time: "But I tell you, if you wish to lay a charge, or give any information, you must do it through me. You can't go upstairs."

"I am not going to give my statement to a — a — " — the little man suddenly noticed the stripes on the sergeant's arm — "to a mere corporal. What I have to say is very important, a matter of life and death. There have been people in the past who have been killed, and I want to prevent more murders. I must see someone at the head of affairs."

Koggel scratched his head, pondered, called a uniformed man over to take his seat, and went into the next room, where he used the telephone.

"It's like this, Inspector," he said, "he refuses to give his statement to me and he says he has information about some murders that have happened and about some that are about to happen. Will you speak to him?"

Joubert said, on inspiration, "I'll hang on. Go and ask him, Sergeant, when these other murders are likely to occur."

He put his hand over the mouthpiece and explained the situation to Rolf and Johnson. "It's just possible," he said, "that we're having a colossal stroke of luck. Maybe it's someone with information about Lereto."

The sergeant's voice scratched over the wire. "Hullo. Hullo, sir."
"Yes?"

"He says the other murders will happen this morning."

"Then send him straight up," said Joubert.

The little man came in under the wing of a uniformed policeman. He took the chair offered to him, and the words came tumbling off his tongue. "I had to see you today," he said. "There may be many people murdered. And there have been murders in the past. I could have come before, only, you see... there were family reasons. My sister — I am afraid my sister is very much involved. But today — well, I felt I could no longer stand by and do nothing any longer. I — "

Joubert said, "All right. Be calm. Let's start right from the beginning, shall we? Get everything down in proper form. First of all, your name?"

"Borgia," said the man, "Cesare Borgia."

❈

Not much time was wasted; within the space of fifteen minutes Doc McGregor was fetched from the magistrate's court, delivered his verdict — "Mad as a coot, but harmless, definitely harmless" — and the man who thought he was the scion of a medieval family was safe in the cells.

"If only," said Joubert, "the Minister had let me do what I wanted and broadcast a general warning to the public to stay away from the central area of the city this morning, I'd have had far less worries."

Johnson asked, "What was his objection?"

"Oh, a dozen reasons. Disrupting commerce, causing panic, creating a situation where Lereto will be afraid to come into the open, and so minimizing our chances of catching him, and so on."

"You know the public," said Rolf. "Would a broadcast warning have had the effect you wanted? Don't you think there would have been more of a headache for you trying to keep everyone out of the area than there is under the present plan?"

"Perhaps, Oom. All the same, it's not very pleasant sitting here, knowing that if all your squads don't work with maximum efficiency, some people stand the chance of being blown to smithereens. And whatever the Minister says, I'll be the one whom the public will blame."

Rolf was thoughtful. "And yet, Dirk, perhaps just by sitting here and thinking, you will solve the problem."

"That's what Lereto says, yes. But why should I believe him?"

"If you believe other things he has said, then why not this? I still feel we haven't gone deeply enough into the matter."

"I've had enough of thought," said Joubert. "What I need now is some action. After all, look at the time. 10.20." He grinned. "Let's say I could concentrate a squad, give them adequate instructions, and take them to the site, all within ten minutes. That would leave exactly half an hour. It took Einstein 30 years to discover a fourth dimension. I don't fancy my chances of finding a fifth in 30 minutes."

"All the same," said Rolf, and he went on speaking, and at that moment, Mr. Lereto, carrying his invention, arrived at the site of his projected experiment. Early, of course, but that was as it should be. No risk of being delayed elsewhere when the City Hall clock struck 11.00. No risk of being unfair to the police...

❂

Constable van Staden of the Railway Police walked the length of platform I and then came back slowly towards the concourse. He looked at his watch, and not for the first time. The hands showed 10.22. All quiet now, but in exactly thirty minutes he and the other constables on duty and all those others who were keeping in the background would have to swoop to clear the station building by 11.00 a.m. In the meantime, his instructions were to look out for a man.

He saw him, standing near the entrance to the ladies waiting room, a thin middle–aged man with greying hair and furtive expression. He was carrying a suitcase.

Van Staden stared at him, and the man caught his stare. He looked about him nervously, put the suitcase down, and moved away a few steps. Van Staden started to walk towards him.

The man moved further away, turned, sidled, and suddenly bolted down the length of platform. He had a good start on the uniformed man but van Staden had won his heat in the 100 yards at the police sports. At the end of the platform he was a mere five yards behind the fugitive.

The man was in an ecstasy of panic. He jumped to the tracks, ran along them, peering white–faced over his shoulder at the pursuer.

There was a train coming, but it was on the next line.

And van Staden still gained, and just as the oncoming train was passing, his reaching fingers tucked in the collar of the man in front.

And the man, teeth bared like a fox, swung round and kicked van Staden in the groin, and he kicked again to loosen his grip and he bucked and skidded and twisted to escape, and somehow he misjudged his distance as he came loose, and he ran straight towards the last coach of the passing train.

To van Staden, contorted in agony on the ground, it seemed the fugitive had managed to stop himself just before the moment of impact, but he knew this was an illusion when the body spun round and toppled and lay looking towards him without a face.

In the meantime, the plainclothes–men who had observed the start of the chase swooped down on the suitcase. They picked it up gingerly, carried it carefully to a car and took it to where the military explosives expert was waiting with his equipment in the centre of a bare expanse of reclaimed foreshore. They gave him the suitcase and retired to a safe distance.

They saw the expert immerse the case in water, and work over it for several minutes. Finally, he brought the suitcase back to the detectives. "Nothing explosive in here," he said.

One of the men, curious, opened the case and began pulling out saturated clothing. At the bottom of the case was a biscuit tin and the lid was closed. He looked up dubiously.

"It's OK," said the expert, "I've had it open already. Nothing dangerous. Funny sort of smell to the stuff, though. What is it, anyway?"

He added the last question because the man had opened the tin and was looking at the contents with familiarity.

"Dagga," said the detective.

❂

Joubert said, "In fact, not only don't I like hanging around doing nothing, I don't see why I have to. I'm going to take over your round, Johnson. You can hang on here in my place."

"But Dirk — "

"Dirk nothing. I'm not your friend this morning. What you've just heard is an order from your superior officer."

Johnson shrugged and grinned resignedly. "Well, if that's the way it's got to be — "

❂

Sergeant Koggel's embarrassed face followed his knock on the door. "Sorry to trouble you, Inspector, but there's another person here who insists on speaking to someone in the C.I.D. A lady."

Joubert said, "Who is it this time? Helen of Troy?"

"No, sir, a Mrs. Stanger. Mrs. Emily Stanger."

"And what in blazes does she want."

"Well, you see, sir, it's like this. She was here about a week ago, and gave a statement to Detective Marais about a handbag of hers that was snatched. Now she wants to add something to the statement. She's seen the man since, and knows where he is working. You see, sir, Marais being away, I thought if you wouldn't mind — "

❂

"You mean she's making your life a misery down there? All right, seeing I'm going out, I don't mind if you do bring her up. Johnson will attend to her." And then, "It's only 10.27 but I'm hoping to leave three minutes ahead of schedule. Are you coming with me, Oom?"

"No," said Rolf.

Johnson said: "That's right. You help me take down this woman's statement. I'll need your moral support."

"You'll have to do without me, I'm afraid. I'm going somewhere where it's quiet, and I'm taking the Lereto dossier with me."

In the open door appeared a uniformed man. With him was a little old lady carrying an umbrella and, with one and the same gesture, she smiled and opened the faucet of her reservoir of words.

Joubert and Rolf escaped.

❂

Joubert went down the stairs, but Rolf le Roux turned into a room down the hall. He put Lereto's letters on the table in front of him, and tried to see beyond the words.

Fifth Dimension... Who, Why, Where, When and — something else.

Lereto was right. There had to be something else.

Analyse it logically. Take the case first of a newspaper report. No, why take a theoretical case — here was a newspaper — take an actual report. This tiny one here, at the bottom of the page. "Late last night" — that was the When — "thieves" — the Who — "broke into the Boston Warehouse in Castle Street" — the Where — "and stole several hundred pounds worth of goods." And the Why was implicit, obviously — the thieves broke in to steal. And there you had a complete report. No, not complete. No mention there of the little things, those little things that must have been there — the psychological trade—marks of the criminals, the way in which they did the crime, the shape, the pattern, the individual touches of method which made it quite distinct from a thousand other cases which the newspaper might describe with the identical Who, Why, Where and When.

The shape...

That's what Lereto must have meant by the fifth dimension. And applied to his problem it means... the shape, too. His own psychological trade—mark. The devil! He said it in his letter: "But even though there are several public buildings... by mentally associating yourself with me, you should be able to deduce... "

Should be able, yes. By finding out the pattern, the shape, of his own mind. By mentally associating...

And the minutes stalked each other around the clock, and each movement of the hands tightened the springs of tension in the minds of the men who watched and waited...

✪

In the Post Office, an elderly man dropped a parcel down a waste paper chute, and was pounced on by the detective on guard. The man squealed his protests, and they were amplified by a woman, who came up almost immediately. The man, she said, was her husband, a model father and grandfather, a pillar of respectability — and if he said that he had not dropped a parcel, then he had not dropped a parcel... A postal employee fished up the bone of contention, and in a panic the man asked to speak privately to the police. In high terror, he told them he had dropped the parcel when he saw his wife approaching. She was a militant pillar of the Temperance Society. If she had investigated the parcel and found it contained sherry —

In the grounds of the House of Assembly, an overzealous detective–constable seized a man with a briefcase, who seemed to him to be acting suspiciously. Fortunately for the detective's future career, his prisoner, the Minister of Justice, had a sense of humour —

To simplify his work, and in a spasm of ingenuity, detec-tive–sergeant Corbett, who was guarding a lane at the back of the art gallery, erected a large poster: NO ADMITTANCE HERE. DANGER. EXPLOSIVES... a little fellow, with a hand–case and a stick and a surreptitious shuffling stride, disregarded the notice. Corbett jumped from concealment, and ran to intercept him. The little man heard him coming, whirled around with his stick upraised. Corbett knocked him out with a single blow and dragged the unconscious form to a nearby Black Maria. En route to Caledon Square, the prisoner came round. He struggled desperately. "You cowards!" he yelled, and then, more quietly, "What do you want with me? I've got no money. I'm just a poor blind man — "

Eight women and four men, members of a religious sect, were

also detained in various public buildings. All had been engaged in leaving, in strategic positions, bundles of copies of a tract entitled The Hour of Doom Approaches —

The hands of the City Hall clock moved on, and the police machine moved into well–oiled action, and they cleared the buildings they were guarding and formed their cordons. But as the first chime of 11.00 rang out, Mr. Lereto, who was where he wanted to be, pressed what he called the trigger of his invention...

✪

And as the first chime of 11.00 rang out, Rolf le Roux saw, in lightning flashes, the truth of the case...

He saw the whole pattern, the egoism, the scrupulous fairness. The phrases and sentences... "Choose your most comfortable chair... the solution will come to you eventually." ... "I have no desire to feed you with information to the extent that you are waiting for me to arrive." Of course! The place. From Lereto's point of view the most public of all public buildings. The building which housed Joubert's most comfortable chair — where he would normally be waiting. Caledon Square.

But where was Lereto?... He pictured the strangers who were on the premises, the drunks in the cells, the man who thought he was Cesare Borgia, the little old lady with the umbrella. "A first–class amateur actor." The umbrella.

The "stick of bombs"...

And while he was thinking this the second chime was ringing out, and he was on his feet and on his way to Joubert's office.

Johnson said, "Phew, that was quite a session," but his voice tailed off. Because of Rolf's face.

The old lady had gone. But the umbrella was still there.

Rolf grabbed it, whirled, and ran for the stairs, and even while he ran his mind clutched at the thought. "It looks so very like... perhaps a mistake... "

And so, because of the doubt in his mind, when he reached the old lady in the doorway of the charge office, he did nothing except bow and hand her the umbrella and say, "You left this behind."

She said, "Thank you," and even in that flash he could not be certain whether the light in her eyes was kindly gratitude or a searching, curious panic.

He stood catching his breath in the doorway, and he watched her walk sedately on the pavement and start to cross Buitenkant Street.

Only, when she reached the centre of the road, she paused and turned. And her turn was not of an old lady in doubt, but of a tiger at bay and she leaned back like a javelin thrower, but the javelin was the umbrella aimed at the doorway.

And in that infinitesimal sub–section of a second, in that instance of poise before action, in that moment of tableau, she was whipped behind a blurt of smoke into another dimension.

The giant hand of the blast slapped Rolf to the ground, and while he was falling the noise came, deafening, and yet behind the deafness, crystal clear and from every direction, he heard the tinkling of glass.

He rose to his feet slowly and he looked over the two parked cars lying on their sides, and he saw there was no great damage except to the street, the mercifully empty street, where a little old lady had once paused in her walk to turn, and where now gaped an angry hole in the ruptured, smoking tarmac.

Postscript

At the time I submitted "The Fifth Dimension" to Ellery Queen's Mystery Magazine, *it had just announced that a panel of critics had voted "The Hands of Mr Ottermole" by Thomas Burke as the finest crime short story ever written. The magazine reprinted the story with a flourish of publicity. The following letter accompanied my own submission — and was eventually printed as a tailpiece to "The Fifth Dimension":*

Dear Ellery,
Please forgive me for taking a leaf out of your own book and providing you with a postscript to the story. It is appropriate to the situation, however, because there is a method, implicit in the narrative, whereby EQMM fans can spot, with absolute certainty and long before Rolf le Roux reaches his own stumbling solution, the disguise assumed by Tom Lereto.

This criminal, informing the police in advance about his crimes is, in effect an inverted Ottermole; and TOM LERETO is an anagram of OTTERMOLE.

Once having spotted this point of identification, the erudite EQMM reader has only to go one step further. In Thomas Burke's famous story, "The Hands of Mr.Ottermole" the criminal (like his inverted namesake in "The Fifth Dimension") has another identity. Throughout the course of Ottermole, the criminal, as you will remember, is referred to as the Sergeant. Now, if the letters making up the word Sergeant are jumbled, another anagram materialises – E. STANGER – or Mrs Emily Stanger.

All in all, I feel justified in saying that "The Fifth Dimension" is 200% fair to EQMM readers.

All my best,

Peter Godfrey

KILL AND TELL

This is a "change of pattern" story – a mystery where all the clues seem to point unerringly in one direction, until suddenly they veer around and you find that they have been indicating something else all the time. This is the only Rolf le Roux tale where all the action is seen through the eyes of a third party – in this case a female secretary.

Bannister called from the study: "Who is it, Miss Jones?" After 12 years of working together he still hadn't got around to calling me by my first name.

I ushered in the three men, repeating their introduction for the benefit of my employer. There was Joubert, the tall C.I.D. Lieutenant; the fresh–looking young detective, Johnson; and the elderly gentleman with the full–blooming moustache and beard, the fiercely glowing pipe. I used his surname, of course — le Roux — but Joubert called him "Rolf."

I used to think Bannister was a handsome man when I first went to work for him, but 12 years is a long time for some people. That day, with his bald patch thrown into relief by the black fringe of hair and heavy horn–rimmed spectacles, he looked like nothing so much as a benign beetle.

I knew, when he asked if I might remain, that his motive was more concerned with the notes I might make than with any courtesy toward me.

The police had no objection to my presence, and Joubert opened the conversation. "You are not entirely a stranger to me, Mr. Bannister," he said. "Although this is the first time I have met you, I have, of course, read your books. The two autographed novels you were kind enough to send to my department when you arrived in Cape Town ultimately found their way to my bookshelf... Certain things in which my department is vitally interested have occurred recently. If you would be prepared to answer some questions, you might help us enormously."

"Fire away," said Bannister.

"The *Province Times* yesterday," Joubert said, carried the story of an interview with you in which you discussed the plot of a novel you have just completed. As I understand it, the book deals with a murder committed by a man who has an unassailable alibi. Is that correct?"

"Fundamentally, yes."

"And I gather from the newspaper report that other than the alibi, there were clear clues pointing in the villain's direction?"

"Yes. In the book, the murderer's wallet with his personal papers is found next to the body, but he is able to prove he was miles away when the fatal shot was fired."

"I take it then that the concoction of an alibi such as you describe in the book would be perfectly feasible in real life?"

"Definitely. And I will go even further, Lieutenant. In real life no amount of police work would ever be able to smash that alibi. In the book, I was forced to adopt a literary subterfuge to make my murderer confess. In real life he would have gone scot–free."

"When did you finish work on your book, Mr. Bannister?"

My employer turned to me. "You completed typing the final chapter of *Murder Elsewhere* on Thursday, didn't you, Miss Jones?"

I said: "Yes — in the morning. I did a couple of final corrections in the afternoon, and I finally sent off the manuscript on the Friday. The registration receipt is on file, if you want to check, but I am perfectly sure."

❂

"Mr. Bannister," Joubert said, "I must warn you at this stage that our visit to you this morning is directly concerned with the investigation of a serious crime. Certain statements you have already made seem to indicate that you are involved. I intend to proceed with this questioning, but I am prepared to wait, if you so desire, until your solicitor arrives."

Bannister's only apparent reaction to this was a raising of the eyebrows.

"This is very unexpected, Lieutenant," he said. "It's a novel experience for me to be a suspect. But a solicitor? No thank you, Lieutenant. My conscience feels particularly clear this morning. What is this serious crime in which you think I'm implicated?"

Joubert said: "Murder."

Bannister's smile broadened, but there was a sober quality in his voice. "Go on," he said.

"You have admitted," said Joubert, "that when you arrived in Cape Town from England, you sent copies of two old books written by yourself to the C.I.D.?"

"Yes."

"Do you remember the titles?"

"Yes. *Death After Hours* and *Tall Man's Murder.*"

Rolf asked the next question. "Tell me, Mr. Bannister," he said, "why did you send these books to the C.I.D.?"

"A custom of mine, Mr. le Roux. I travel a lot, as you know, and whenever I reach a centre in which I intend to stay for a while, I send copies of these two books to the police. A sort of tribute," he added with a grin: "to people who supply me with the raw material of my craft."

"But why those two books particularly?" Rolf persisted.

"If you examine them," said Bannister, "you will notice a newspaper clipping pasted to the fly–leaf of each. That's the explanation — both books were based on actual cases — unsolved cases — and I assumed they would be of some interest to the C.I.D."

Joubert again took over the questioning. "We noticed the clippings, of course, and there are certain curious features about both. The one pasted on the fly–leaf of *Death After Hours* is the report on the inquest on William Cullingworth, who died from the effects of potassium cyanide poisoning at Ipswich almost 15 years ago. The strange feature of the case was that Cullingworth was discovered in a locked room; there was no trace of poison except in the deceased; nor was the container of that poison ever found. There was no evidence of foul play. The last person to see him alive was yourself, but you had left him at least an hour before death occurred, as estimated by the pathologist. Since potassium cyanide is an almost instantaneous poison, and you were with a group of people from the moment you left Cullingworth, your alibi was unassailable."

"Go on, Lieutenant."

"Exactly six months after Cullingworth's death, the book on the case was first published. Rather quick work that, wasn't it?"

Bannister smiled again. "I'm a fast writer, Lieutenant," he said.

"Yes? Well, that may be. At any rate, the story revealed an

ingenious method of administering poison by means of a delayed–action capsule. The murdered man in the book, you called Battista, but he was obviously Cullingworth. Just as obviously the murderer, whom you called Crafford, was yourself."

❂

Bannister laughed. "Don't tell me the crime you are investigating is poor old Cullingworth's death? Isn't Ipswich a bit outside your jurisdiction?"

"Yes, Mr. Bannister," Rolf said, "but what happened at Ipswich may be relevant to the case we are working on now. What interests me is why, in the story, you made yourself the murderer?"

"There's nothing mysterious about it," Bannister said. "It arises naturally from the type of detective story I write. The general formula of my books is the commission of a crime which cannot be solved by ordinary police routine — only by the irregular methods of Triton Drake, my detective character. Can you wonder that I identify myself with the murderers in my books? In the case of Cullingworth the empathy was total. I had spoken to the man only a short while before his mysterious death. I asked myself the question: Assuming I had killed Cullingworth, how did I do it? The answer was *Death After Hours*. Of course, as good a case could be made out to establish my identity with Triton Drake."

"I take it," said Rolf, "that you also identified with the killer in *Tall Man's Murder?*"

"Yes," answered Bannister. "I knew the victim of the actual crime — in fact, we were in the same picnic party the day he met his death. The murderer was never discovered, although the weapon was found — a piece of steel fencing post about 18 inches long.

"What gave me the idea for the book was the medical evidence at the inquest. The medical examiner was positive, on account of the angle of the blow, that the murderer was over six feet tall. As you can see, I am several inches shorter than that, and again I asked myself the question: Assuming you are the murderer, how would it be possible for you to fake the angle of the blow to provide yourself with an alibi? After a few minutes thought I found the answer — a ridiculously simple one. So I wrote the book."

"And what was this ridiculously simple answer?" Joubert asked.

"It struck me that the doctor's deduction was illogical. What he should have said was that the murderer's height from the ground was well over six feet at the moment the blow was struck. A wound of the identical angle could have been struck by a shorter man standing on something at the time. Since the scene of the crime was flat terrain, with no stones or logs handy, I conceived the idea of a meticulous murderer, after premeditation, jumping into the air to deliver the blow. Incidentally, the method is perfectly practical — it's simply a matter of correct timing."

"You sound as though you had experimented," said Joubert, with a mirthless grin.

"Oh, but I did," said Bannister, and the irony in his voice matched Joubert's tone. "Of course, I did not use a human subject — just a soft cushion balanced on a hat–rack."

✪

Joubert opened a notebook. "I see here," he said, "that the book was published only four months after the actual crime was committed. That was even quicker work than last time, wasn't it?"

"It was an easier plot to handle," said Bannister, almost sweetly, and then suddenly flared up. "What nonsense is this, anyway? I've agreed to answer your questions, but I doubt if you've any right to interrogate me without informing me first about what crime you're investigating. And what relevance can the speed of my writing have?"

"It has some importance," said Joubert, and turned abruptly to me. "How long have you been employed by Mr. Bannister, Miss Jones?"

I told him.

"That's a pity," he went on. "That means you came to work for him only after the publication of *Tall Man's Murder*."

Bannister's voice was now cold with rage. "This is going too far, Lieutenant. My agreement to answer questions didn't include a cross–examination of my secretary. Beyond typing my manuscripts and taking dictation from me, she can have no possible knowledge... "

Before I could stop myself, anger and hatred leapt into my voice. "That's not true, Mr. Bannister," I said, "although you probably don't know it. You don't work for a person as long as I've worked for you without learning plenty about him — sometimes more than he knows about himself."

Immediately I regretted losing my temper. "I'm sorry," I said more quietly. "You see, Mr. Bannister, it's obvious to both of us that the police are making some kind of mistake. If so, there can be no harm done if I answer their questions. In fact, it may help in rectifying the error more quickly."

Bannister said nothing.

Joubert went on. "Isn't four months, Miss Jones, a remarkably short time between starting a book and final publication?"

"It is fast," I said, "but not unduly so. Once Mr. Bannister has the idea worked out in his mind he dictates very rapidly."

Joubert turned again to my employer. He said: "In this latest book of yours *Murder Elsewhere* I gather that as usual the murderer is modelled upon yourself?"

"And the detective," said Bannister.

Joubert conceded the point. "Yes, and the detective. Who were the other characters in real life? The man who was murdered, for instance?"

"I don't see the significance of this," Bannister said, "but the character was based on Blair Clayton, a wholesale merchant here in Cape Town."

"I know Clayton," said Joubert. "Didn't you have some sort of a scene with him at the Delmonico about six weeks ago?"

"As a matter of fact there was some trouble," Bannister said. "Clayton had had a few drops too many; there was an argument, and he struck me. I couldn't hit a drunken man, and I had no desire to make an exhibition of myself in a public place, so I simply walked out."

"Isn't it a fact that the quarrel you had with Clayton concerned a woman?"

My employer's voice trembled with anger. "Once again, Lieutenant, you are abusing your position. I've agreed to answer any question relevant to this mysterious case you are investigating. I have not agreed to answer irrelevant queries of a purely personal nature."

"Your quarrel with Clayton," said Joubert, "is extremely relevant to the case I am investigating. I must tell you, too, that I have other evidence."

Bannister gave him a hunted look. "If others have told you what the quarrel was about, then the damage has already been done. I don't suppose any further harm will ensue by confirming your allegation. Yes, Lieutenant, a woman was involved. However, I would appreciate it if the name of the lady could be kept out of any publicity. Clayton, as everyone knows, is the world's worst philanderer. When I saw him at his usual game with a lady of whom I am very fond, I tried to warn him off at the Delmonico. What now? Has he had the impudence to file charges of assault against me?"

Joubert made some sort of signal to Johnson, who handed him an envelope. Out of it he took a gold tie-pin.

"This has your initials on it," he said to Bannister. "I don't suppose you'll deny it's yours?"

Bannister seemed more pleased than otherwise to see the pin. "Certainly not," he said. "I've been looking for it everywhere. Where and when was it found?"

"At three o'clock this morning" said Joubert grimly, "beside the murdered body of Blair Clayton."

❂

I've never seen my employer so taken aback, but it was only for a moment, then a glint of amusement appeared in his eyes. "Many things are clearer to me now," he said, and added: "I take it then, Lieutenant, that Clayton was killed some time during last night?"

"As near as we can make it," said Joubert, "he was murdered between 10 p.m. and 1 a.m."

Bannister laughed. "Then I'm afraid you'll have to look elsewhere for the guilty party, he said. "I can account for every moment of my time between those hours."

Joubert said: "So could the killer in *Murder Elsewhere.*"

Bannister lost his temper. "To blazes with you and your innuendos!" he said. "If you feel I am the guilty man, then arrest me and charge me with the crime. If you are not ready to do that, then get out of my house!"

Joubert bristled in turn. "It is perfectly true that I have no direct facts to prove you murdered Clayton, but you have failed to take into consideration the value of circumstantial evidence. Listen to me: When there are sufficient circumstances forming a pattern of guilt, any jury anywhere in the world will convict."

Bannister started to say something, but Joubert raised his voice to continue inexorably, "I'll show the jury that you hated Clayton, that you came to blows with him recently, that your tie–pin was found next to his body. You will have an alibi, but I will show them your own description of how that alibi was constructed, of how the murder was done, written by you in your book at least a week before Clayton was killed.

"I'll tell them also of the other two violent deaths that have occurred in the past, and how books on these deaths were published a remarkably short time after the murders have occurred. When I have accentuated that point, the jurymen will ask themselves: 'Were those books written before or after the crimes?'

"They will want to know in more detail exactly what kind of man you are — and I am going to tell them. An intelligent man, yes, but with a mental twist causing you to commit almost perfect crimes to baffle the police, and glorify your own opinion of yourself. They will see clearly — as I have seen — how you gloat over the fact that you kill, tell the world with only indirect concealment how you have killed, and then get off scot–free. Only, you are not going to escape this time. You remembered all the facts, but forgot the total pattern."

"There are other patterns, Dirk," said Rolf le Roux. "You mustn't arrest this man. He is innocent."

Joubert was completely taken aback. "Can you convince a jury of that?" he asked, with a touch of sarcasm.

Rolf said, quietly: "You have stressed Bannister's intelligence. Can you honestly believe that an intelligent man would scheme a murder, write a book about it, and then give the details of the crime to a newspaper before the murder is committed?"

Joubert tried to press his original point. "But the facts, Rolf, the facts! You must admit Clayton's murder was an exact duplicate of the crime committed in *Murder Elsewhere*, as told to a newspaper interviewer. True, only the bare details of the method used were given to the *Province Times*. Who but Bannister could have provided such an exact copy in real life?"

Rolf said: "His secretary."

When my voice came, it was as though I was listening to another person. "Are you accusing me of murder, Mr. le Roux? What motive could I possibly have for doing away with Mr. Clayton?"

"Revenge," said Rolf, and went on quickly before I could interrupt. "No, let me explain. I began to wonder when you rounded on Mr. Bannister. There was hate in your voice and your expression, and I asked myself why such an efficient girl works 12 years with a person she hates. The obvious reason is that you didn't always hate him, and the intensity of your present feeling made me suspect that your original emotions were just as intense. I say that you stayed with Mr. Bannister for the major portion of the period because you were in love with him."

"This is ridiculous," I heard myself saying. "If I was in love with Mr. Bannister why did I continue to work for him when I started to hate him?"

❂

He said: "I don't think the transition was instantaneous — I think it took place slowly over a number of years, going from love to frustration, to sadness, to dislike and, finally hatred. I feel the last stage only came when you were deceived by still another man, and suddenly realised the years you had wasted."

My voice said: "Who was this mythical man with whom I'm supposed to have fallen in love?"

"Blair Clayton — and that's not entirely guesswork, Miss Jones. Clayton called here often; he must have spoken with you many times. He had the reputation of making love to every woman he fancied. You are an attractive lady, Miss Jones — why should you be the one exception in his life?"

I did not answer.

"When Clayton deceived you," he went on, "I think you were filled with bitter loathing of both men who had caused you so much frustration. And then, when Bannister grew to hate Clayton, and dictated to you details of a perfect plot for his murder, you saw a chance of revenge against both men."

Joubert interrupted, uneasily: "This is not evidence, Oom. Your reasoning is plausible, but we could never get a conviction on it."

"I agree," said Rolf, "but with that alternative pattern brought forward, you could never get a conviction against Bannister either."

"Come now, Mr. le Roux," interrupted Bannister, "while I appre—

ciate the building up of a hypothetical case to get me out of trouble, aren't you being a bit hard on Miss Jones? After all, I know her — "

This goaded me. "What do you know about me?" I asked. "You — who have always looked on me as a piece of office equipment? That man discovered more about me in less than an hour than you have seen in the 12 years we have worked together. Oh yes, everything he said was true — I killed Clayton because I hated him and I hated you...

"I was in love with you when I first joined you. Everything you did was right when I made plot suggestions to you, and you rejected them, and then came forward with the identical ideas as your own brilliant inspirations, I wasn't annoyed. I saw you had forgotten my part and I was proud to have helped you even so indirectly. But that changed. Gradually I came to realise that you were a thief — you had stolen my love, you had stolen my brains, you had stolen my youth.

"At the time I met Blair Clayton, these things didn't count for much. Later, when I realised I might have held him had I met him 12 years earlier, I saw for the first time just how much they mattered.

"Now think back and realise the extent to which I influenced you towards your own doom: The sending of the books of previous cases to the police, touches in the plot of *Murder Elsewhere* that suited my own purpose better, yes — even persuaded you to give the interview to the newspaper. They won't hang you, Bannister — they'll hang me instead. But I don't care. I have very little to live for, anyway. And I won't entirely lose my revenge.

"Do you know what my last thought will be on the gallows? I'll be thinking of you, conscious of yourself at last as a colossal sham, as a vulture battening on the brains of others, as the person morally responsible for two deaths — Blair's and mine. I'll be thinking of you, hating yourself — and I'll die happy, Bannister — do you hear that? Happy!"

AND TURN THE HOUR

This is my own favourite "time" story. What I like most about it is the sinister atmosphere of the incredible shift of time, the incomprehensibility of the clues, the tortuous accuracy of the deductions, and the simple and rational understanding in the final section of the tale.

The world smiled... it was warm, and its warmth prickled through his eyelids, behind his eyes, and there was another warmth inside that prickled up to meet it. An excitement, a lazy grasshopper springing of memories. The money, first. No more grind, no more debt, no more working for other people. And then Heath. Yes, Heath in his arms, her eyes bright but her lower lip tremulous in the ecstasy of saying yes. Last night. Wonderful night. And now the sun was shining.

He bought a new watch. On impulse. There was some sort of symbolism there, but nothing deep. New life — new watch. He came out of the shop like a schoolboy on holiday, unstrapping the old watch, dropping it carefully into his left–hand trouser pocket. He put the new one on his wrist, and adjusted the hands to conform with the clock in the tower of the City Hall. 10.55. He started to wind.

A vague cloud passed through his mind. He should have wound first, of course. Maybe a minute... He looked at the City Hall clock again, and then down at his wrist. 11.47. And they both gave the same time.

He felt a sudden nausea, and then his mind reeled in a drunken clutch of hope. This was his old watch on his wrist. He must have put the new one in his pocket. A mistake of some kind...

His hand reached into his pocket, fingers groping, pulling out the contents. He looked. An unused cinema ticket and a crushed white flower trembled in his palm. He had never seen them before. The warmth behind his eyelids turned into a shaft of cold.

✪

"And that is all he can remember," said Dr Beresky. He shook his lined head gently and his large ears trembled. Then he added: "I am very worried about him."

Rolf le Roux leaned forward sympathetically, and held his pipe for a moment away from his beard. "I still don't understand," he said, "why you have come to me."

Beresky answered his question only obliquely. He said, "Let me tell you something about amnesia. First it is brought on by a trauma — a shock. Second, when an amnesia victim visits a psychiatrist, he already wants to be cured, and so he is well on the way to curing himself. All I have to do is show him the right road." He cleared his throat. "Young Winter came to me of his own accord, it is true, but there are still undeniable signs that he does not wish to be cured. Yes, I say that even though he is tortured by the idea that without a cure he will go mad, that he will lose the girl to whom he has just become engaged, and all the benefits of the large sum of money he has just inherited."

Rolf asked: "Have you any idea why he does not want to be cured?"

"Yes, but only in very general terms. I can say, with some certainty that he does not want to remember what happened in the missing fifty–two minutes because the event or events which caused the shock are too unpleasant for him to face... " He hesitated. "That much one can say of amnesia generally, but in Winter's case the resistance to remembering is so strong that the cause must have been something... unthinkable."

Rolf prompted again: "And you have come to me?"

"Because you live in the same lodging–house as Winter, and he is fond of you and has confidence in you. Perhaps you can help break down his resistance. And then again, you have a connection with the police."

"In what way is that useful?"

"Mr. le Roux, if it would only be possible for us to find out where Winter went during the missing period, exactly what he did — "

Rolf said, "That may be more difficult than you think. After all, the trail is five days old. But I am quite prepared to try."

"Thank you," said Beresky, and hesitated again. "Perhaps the police would know of some incident, which happened during that time, which Winter might have seen or been involved in. If so — "

"It is worth looking into, Dr. Beresky, but anything violent would certainly have got into the newspapers, and I have seen nothing there. No, but there are other things which may help. Let us see. We know certain details about the period. We know that at the outside something happened to destroy Winter's balance of mind. We know that he was in Plein Street or the immediate vicinity at the time. We know that after he did certain things — he rid himself of the new watch and put the old one on his wrist, and he acquired a cinema ticket and a flower, a white lily. These things, I should imagine, must bear some relationship to the shock which caused the mental imbalance?"

"Definitely."

"And in your treatment you yourself have discovered nothing more about any of these individual items?"

"Nothing that sheds any real light on the matter to me. But perhaps if you... Look, Mr. le Roux, I will be treating Winter at 2.30 this afternoon. If you would like to be present, it might be a helpful influence. As things stand, I do not see what harm it could do. Personally, I am at a dead end."

"I would very much like to come, " said Rolf.

❂

The call from Detective–Sergeant Johnson came while Rolf was still in the waiting room of the nursing home.

"Nothing," said Johnson. "No complaints at all from the vicinity of Plein Street — in fact, there was no crime of violence at all in Cape Town during daylight hours of that day. There was a fight between some drunken sailors at the bottom of Adderley Street just after 6 pm but I don't suppose that qualifies."

Rolf said: "No, The Incident, whatever it was, must have occurred near Plein Street between say 10.45 and noon. And it must have been sufficiently horrible to make a normal youngster lose his memory. That's all I can tell you at the moment. Perhaps this afternoon... I will get in touch with you later. And what about street accidents? Have you checked them?"

"Yes. No luck there either. Still, there may have been one unreported. I'll try the hospitals for you this afternoon, Oom. Will you give me a ring at Caledon Square just before 5?"

As Rolf hung up, Dr. Beresky came bustling up. He shook hands. "I am sorry to have kept you waiting, " he said, "but I am quite ready now. Will you come this way?"

Rolf followed him down the cream–coloured passage.

Donald Winters lay fully dressed on a couch in the room. He looked up as they entered, but slowly, as though his muscles were rustily responding to habit, and his thoughts were somewhere in the distance.

"Your old friend, Mr. le Roux is here," said Beresky. "He is trying to help us."

Winters said: "Hullo, Oom." Again it was a slow reflex action; his voice was expressionless, unmeaning. All the same, in brief tantalysing flashes, panic chased hope across his eyes. Rolf thought of those eyes as he had last seen them — alert and full of fun. He took one of the chairs at the side of the couch, Beresky took the other. He rolled up the boy's right sleeve, found a vein, and inserted the needle of a hypodermic syringe. He explained: "I am injecting sodium pentothol, a hypnotic drug. It helps release the inhibitions. Donald, will you please start counting?"

Winters said: "One, two, three, four... five... shix... " His voice blurred sleepily. Beresky ceased his slow pressure on the plunger. He started to talk, slowly and distinctly.

"Donald, think back to when you were walking down Plein Street. You were very happy because you had inherited money and had just become engaged. You passed a jeweller's shop, turned in, and bought a watch. Then what did you do?"

"I put... the new... on wrist... the old in... pocket."

"And then?"

"Adjust time. With clock. Wind watch."

"Go on."

"Looked at clock again. Time... had changed."

Beresky said: "Listen carefully. Time doesn't change. Hours don't vanish into thin air. Between the times the clock changed, you did things, saw things. You know that, don't you?"

The boy on the couch moved his head from side to side. He groaned. Beresky persisted: "You know that, don't you? Answer me."

The boy said: "God, leave... alone." His left hand started to clench and unclench. He whimpered.

"What was it you did, Donald? What was it you saw?"

The boy gritted his teeth, jerked his head aside in a parody of violence.

"What did you do? What did you see?"

Winter tried weakly to pull his right wrist out of Beresky's grasp. He flexed his knees, rolled his head. He opened his mouth as though he was going to shout, but the voice that emerged was barely a whisper: "No."

✪

Beresky mopped his forehead. "All right, boy," he said, "I won't ask you again. Not now, anyway. Relax. That's right. Nobody's going to hurt you. Good. Now we're going to have another little experiment. You won't even have to think, this time. When I ask you a question, just tell me what comes into your mind. Ready?"

"Yes."

"Then here's the first word: Watch?"

The boy hardly hesitated. "Life."

"Don't just answer with a single word," said Beresky. "Tell me everything that comes into your mind. Now, let's try again: Flower?"

"Verse."

"Go on."

"Flower. Verse. White. Pure." The next two words then came bursting from his lips: "No blood!"

"All right, Donald. Easy, now. Think of a special kind of flower. A lily. That's your word — lily."

Winters said, "Lily... of Laguna. Lagoon. Sea. Muizenberg. Sand, white sand. White hand." He began to move his head again.

Beresky pressed him: "White hand?"

The boy moaned.

"White?"

"Clean. Pure."

"Hand?"

The boy screamed.

❁

Beresky came with Rolf out into the sunlight. The psychiatrist said, "You see now what I mean when I say the shock he experienced must have been horrible. And violent."

"Horror is relative," said Rolf. "The simplest acts may have an element of horror to a specific individual. I, for example, hate to kill spiders... it is a question of a particular type of upbringing and personal experiences. But you are right — what shocked the hour loose from Winter's life is associated with violence. With the shedding of blood. And yet there were no crimes of violence that day."

"Are you certain of that?"

"Almost certain. I shall know definitely tonight... look, Doctor, doesn't Winter's fianceé live near here? Maybe she can help."

"Miss Cooper? I've already spoke to her, and I doubt if... but perhaps you may discover something. She lives about four blocks down. That big apartment building on the left side of the road."

"I will find it," said Rolf, and then: "Goodbye, Doctor, I will telephone you tomorrow."

❁

The apartment building was ultra modern, all chrome and glass, and the girl who answered his ring was refreshing in her naturalness. She wore her hair long and loose, and dressed with that artless simplicity which is the truest smartness. She had been crying.

Rolf introduced himself, explained the purpose of his visit. She said: "Oh yes, Mr. le Roux. Donald has often spoken of you. Come inside, please. This is my brother, Arthur."

The sullen, powerfully–built man stood up, extended a perfunctory hand in greeting. "Sorry I can't stay," he said, and then: "If you're going to talk about Winters, I can't be of any use." His voice was both unpleasant and impatient. He went out.

Heath Cooper said: "Tell me, Mr. le Roux, is Donald any better?"

Rolf shook his head. "No, Miss Cooper. But I think you may be able to help him."

She said impulsively: "I feel I've known you for a long time. Call me Heath. I will call you Oom." And then: "What can I do? Dr. Beresky won't even let me see him."

Rolf took a deep pull at his pipe. "Let me explain. Donald has lost his memory because of some deep shock he experienced this morning. If I can find out what caused that shock... "

She shook her head helplessly. "I didn't see him at all, Oom. I had an appointment with my dressmaker. We had arranged to meet in the afternoon, but of course... "

"And you can think of nothing that might have put him in a state of mind where a shock might have been accentuated? Did you get the impression that he was worried? Think hard, Heath."

"Nothing, Oom. All his worries had gone. He'd just inherited his money. We'd just become engaged. We were both very happy. More happy, I suppose, than most couples, because... well, if it hadn't been for the money, Donald would never have asked me to marry him."

"Why not?"

"Well, probably on account of my brother — really my half–brother, Oom. He and Donald don't like each other, as you might have noticed. Arthur's a rich man, and he supports me. Donald didn't realise I'd cheerfully have given everything up just to be with him. He had some silly pride that made him keep silent until he could afford to give me everything that Arthur... But, of course, the inheritance cleared up that barrier."

"I see. And how long have you known Donald?"

"Just over a year."

"And did he talk freely to you about his past life?"

"Yes. He's a very frank sort of person, Oom. I think he's told me... most things."

Rolf said: "I am going to mention a few words. See if any of them strikes a chord in connection with anything Donald has ever told you. Concentrate. I'll say them slowly."

"I'm ready."

"Right, here they are then: Flower. Muizenberg. Hand. Blood."

She leaned forward in bewilderment. "Nothing, Oom, nothing."

The tears were in her eyes again.

❂

Rolf looked at his watch as he came out of the apartment building, and walked briskly to a taxi–rank. He gave the driver the address of the lodgings. Once there, he spoke persuasively to the proprietor, got from him a key, and let himself into the boy's room.

For a moment he stood irresolute. In his mind he heard Beresky say 'Flower' and the blurred voice answer 'Verse'. He moved to the bookcase.

There were two volumes of poetry, one by William Morris and the other by Kipling. He took both books to the table. He thought of going through them for an hour or so; then he remembered an old trick. He allowed both books to fall open naturally. The William Morris book fell open at "The Haystack in the Floods." Before reading, he turned his eyes to the Kipling volume, and suddenly prickled in discovery. On the page that faced him was a poem called "The Flowers."

He read it through carefully, word by word. Then with the stem of his pipe, he scored the page next to the third verse:

"Buy my English posies!
  You that will not turn –
Buy my hot–wood clematis,
  Buy a frond o' fern
Gathered where the Erskine leaps
  Down the road to Lorne –
Buy my Christmas creeper
  And I'll say where you were born!
West away from Melbourne dust holidays begin –
They that mock at Paradise woo at Cora Lynn –
Through the great South Otway gums sings the great South Main –
Take the flower and turn the hour, and kiss your love again!"

In his mind Rolf began to see the dim outline of a pattern and he did not like what he saw. He went over the words again. Royal

Heath, he said to himself, and then Heath and lilies. The word white leaped at him from the context. He remembered the boy's association — pure — and he saw again Heath Cooper and the appeal in her eyes. And he remembered the boy's next words, "No blood!"

He said aloud, " 'Take the flower and turn the hour, and kiss your love again,' " and then, " 'And turn the hour, and kiss... ' "

The pattern began to take shape.

He took the volume with him, locked the door, and went down the passage, to his own room. He sat by the telephone for some time before he dialed. He asked for Johnson.

"That you, Oom? No luck at all. No hospital cases unreported — "

"No, that's all right, Johnson. There's something else, now. This boy's name is Donald Winter — make a note of that. I want you to find out if there's any record of him being involved in a murder case some time in the past. Wait, I can give you more details. The murder was one where the victim bled a lot, and it must have happened over a year ago."

On his way to Caledon Square, Rolf stopped off at the post office. He looked at the long rank of flower stalls, alive with colour and rubbed his beard contemplatively.

An old woman brandished a fragrant bunch under his nose. "Only two shillings, Master," she said.

She looked bright eyed and intelligent. "I have ten shillings for you," said Rolf, "if you can find me the flowerseller who sold one white lily to a young man last Friday morning, and there will be another ten shillings for this person."

"Yes, Master." She bustled off, talking to this stallholder and that. In a short while she was back with a man who eyed Rolf suspiciously. He said: "I sold a young man a white lily last Friday morning. What does the Master want to know?"

"Everything you can tell me about it."

"He asked for a lily and I sold it to him. That is all." The man was very uncomfortable. He was holding his left hand very firmly in his pocket.

On inspiration, Rolf said: "I am not from the police, and you may keep the watch." He took out an additional note, and the Coloured man thawed visibly.

He said: "I think the young man was mad. He did not want a

bunch of flowers. He said he must have just one lily, and it must be pure white. I found one and he gave me a shilling for it. Then I saw him standing on the corner, and he squashed the lily in his hand and put it in his pocket. I did not see him after that."

Rolf handed over the notes. He prompted: "And what about the watch?"

"He had two watches, Master, an old one and a new one. He was holding them both in his left hand while he was talking to me. After he crushed the flower, he put the old watch back on his wrist and dropped the new one in the gutter. I picked it up. If the young master had come back, I..."

"It is all right," said Rolf. "He does not want it any more."

Round the corner, in Plein Street, he took the cinema ticket from his wallet, and showed it at the box–office where it had been purchased. The hard blonde gave a cursory glance at it, and spoke before he could say anything. "No returns. You should have gone in when you bought the ticket."

"This is not my ticket," said Rolf. "I am from the police and I am making certain enquiries. Do you remember selling this ticket to a young man last Friday morning?"

"Mister," said the blonde, "I sell five hundred tickets to young men every morning, and if you line them all up in front of me five minutes later, I still wouldn't be able to swear to any one of them."

Rolf persisted: "But this young man did not go into the cinema. Don't you remember anything about that?"

"I wouldn't, but Jimmy might. Jimmy!"

The uniformed man at the door came over. Rolf explained again.

"Come to think of it," said Jimmy, "I do remember something. Young guy with fair hair?"

"Yes."

"Well, he acted a bit screwy. He bought the ticket all right, and then came over to look at the poster. We had a featurette on that day, which was also advertised — a 'Crime Does Not Pay' short — and he seemed to be peering at the announcement. All of a sudden he just walked away."

Do you remember the feature film?"

"Last Friday? Wait a minute. Abbott and Costello... no, that was on Thursday only. Roy Rogers was on at the beginning of the

week. I've got it — Burt Lancaster."
"And the title of the picture?"
"*Kiss the Blood off my Hands.*"

✪

The pattern was balanced, complete. Except for the murder.
And Johnson got hold of the particulars.

It had happened 27 months before. The victim was a young
man named Clyde Parsons, and his throat had been cut in the
dining room of his apartment in Fresnaye. There were signs of a
slight struggle; Parsons had been forced back onto a table before
the murderer could effect the lethal cut. The weapon was left on
the floor, but it had been wiped clean of fingerprints. Blood was
all over the room.

And Donald Winters?

"Clyde Parsons was a great friend of mine," Winters had said
in his statement, "and I was in the habit of letting myself into his
apartment without knocking. I did not have a key and the door
was always locked when Parsons was out. On the evening of
August 17, at approximately eight p.m. I called round at Parson's
rooms. I could hear the radio playing inside and the door was
unlocked, so I was surprised not to find any lights burning. I had
just turned on the switch when I was struck over the head and
lost consciousness. I recovered consciousness only two hours later
under the care of the police surgeon... No, I did not see the person
who struck me. All I saw before I was struck was a hand covered
with blood, holding an iron poker. Apart from the blood, I am
unable to remember whether there was anything distinctive
about the hand, but I do have the feeling that there was some
abnormality about it which I have forgotten, and which I will
recognise if I ever see the hand again... Yes, Parsons was very
popular and to the best of my knowledge he had no enemies.
However, when I had seen him the day before, he had mentioned
he had worries in connection with someone called Prentice."

With his thumbnail Johnson underlined the last sentence.
"And this name, Oom," he said, "is the most interesting feature of
the whole case."

"Why so?"

"We've heard of it in other connections. Nothing definite, you understand. Scraps of reported conversations, and a couple of anonymous letters, but enough to convince us that this Prentice, whoever he or she may be, is a very remarkable blackmailer."

"Why do you say Prentice may be a woman?"

"Well, there's nothing in our information to indicate gender, so I'm covering every contingency. Besides, I've always found women turn more readily to blackmail than men."

Rolf grinned. "It seems to me you know the wrong type of women," he said. "But seriously, I think we can find Prentice for you. Only there will be no evidence."

"Yes? But will there be any possible grounds which might justify a temporary arrest?"

"I think so."

"Then you needn't worry about evidence. If I can show Prentice under lock and key to a certain woman, and promise her complete anonymity, then she'll talk. And we'll also hear from some of the others. When can we make the arrest?"

Rolf said, "Tomorrow morning, I think — I will telephone you tonight with details. But you will have to promise to do exactly as I say. There are more things at stake than the arrest of a murderer, I'm afraid... "

He left then, taking the bus and the long walk back to his room, because he had much to think over.

But before he caught the bus, he telephoned Heath. And he chose the telephone booth on the corner of Plein Street, near the jeweller's shop where Donald Winters had bought his watch.

He asked her questions, and knew the answers before she gave them.

"Yes, Oom. My dressmaker has a room in a building on the corner of Plein Street. Murray House. She's on the second floor. And yes, we did stand talking on the balcony for quite a while."

In his room, Rolf thought again of the problem and its two aspects — the past and the future. The past he knew, every twist and nook and cranny, but when he thought of the future, his mind was shadowy, groping. It was possible that success on the one side would lead to disaster on the other. He did not know enough to decide such a momentous matter for himself. It was a decision for a specialist.

Regretfully, he decided it would be better if he shared his information. He hoped Dr. Beresky would approve his plan.

He reached stubby fingers for the telephone directory.

✪

The bell was pressed long and loud. The time was seven in the morning.

Inside there was a muttered curse and then the door was opened violently by a man in pajamas and dressing gown. There were traces of shaving lather on his face. He said: "What in hell do you want?"

The fresh–complexioned man standing in the forefront of the group asked: "Mr. Arthur Cooper?"

"Yes?"

"I am Detective–Sergeant Johnson of the Cape Town C.I.D. I believe you know Mr. le Roux, Dr. Beresky and Mr. Winters, I am sorry that we have got you up so early in the morning but we were anxious to find both you and your sister at home. There is an urgent matter to discuss."

Cooper hesitated, then said ungraciously: "Well, come in."

They filed into the living room.

Heath was there, also in a dressing gown. She said, "Donald!" and made as though to go to him, but Beresky's expression stopped her. She sidled into a chair and looked at the boy. He did not look at her. His actions were slow and mechanical, and his eyes were afraid.

Cooper said: "Well, come on. What is this urgent business?"

Johnson looked at Rolf, who said: "I will explain." He settled himself in a chair, and his eyes moved from Cooper to Winters to Heath.

He said: "You all know that Donald is suffering from amnesia. There is an hour missing out of his life. The investigation of what happened in that hour has led back to a murder which was committed over two years ago. Donald was a witness. He walked into the victim's rooms before the murderer had left and was knocked unconscious. All he saw was a blood–stained hand holding a poker just before he was hit. But there was something about the hand that made him know he would recognise it if he saw it again. Some sort of physical difference to other hands. And a physical difference that was not apparent normally, but only when the hand was gripping something."

"What has that got to do with us?" said Cooper, impatiently.

"I will tell you," said Rolf. "The morning when Donald fell ill, he looked at a balcony, and saw a hand gripping the railing. It was a hand with the same infirmity as the one which had gripped the poker on the night of the murder. When he saw to whom the hand belonged, his mind was upset."

Heath asked, "Whose hand was it, Oom?"

Rolf looked at her steadily. He said, "Yours."

Only the boy did not look at her. He stared intently at the far corner, and his face was twisted in uncomprehending misery.

Heath started to say, "Oh, no, I — " and then Arthur Cooper interrupted fiercely. "What nonsense is this? Winters, is this the story you have told them?"

The boy's eyes twitched in panic.

Rolf said, "He has told us nothing. He still does not remember anything. But it is the only explanation of the facts. He lost his memory because he associated his fiancee with the murderer of his best friend."

Cooper laughed suddenly. "Don't worry, Heath." He turned again to Rolf. "What sort of a case do you think you are building up? Heath wouldn't harm a fly. Even if Winter did confirm your imaginative reasoning — and that is all it can be — even if he did confirm it, I say, it would prove nothing. He made a mistake."

"He did make a mistake," said Rolf. "His fiancee didn't murder Clyde Parsons. She couldn't have. The crime could not have been committed by a woman of Heath's physique. A man did it, a man powerful enough to overpower a strong victim, force him backward on to a table, and then cut his throat."

Cooper looked shocked. "Then why this picking on Heath — ?"

"Just because Donald did make a mistake. Because of the abnormality in the hand. An abnormality which would be an impossible coincidence if shared between her and some stranger — but one which might be perfectly natural in a blood relative."

Heath suddenly buried her face in her hands. The boy's expression did not change. Johnson licked his lips.

Cooper blustered, "Have you now got the impudence to accuse

me?"

"Yes. But you can easily prove your innocence if you want to. Are you prepared to grip this length of wood I have here, and let Heath grip it too, so we can compare results?"

"No," said Cooper, and laughed again. "Why should I submit myself to a test which is based entirely on theory — a theory unconfirmed even by the man you say provided the basis of it? No, I will not do it, and you cannot compel me to. Nor are you in a position to hold me on suspicion."

"That is quite true," said Rolf, meekly, and added: "But there is one other theory on which I am prepared to stand or fall. You see, Mr. Cooper, the name of the murderer is known. It is the same name as the mysterious person who makes a living from blackmail. It is obviously not his real name, and yet there must have been a reason for his choosing it."

Cooper said sarcastically, "What alias am I supposed to have adopted? And what tortuous reason have you concocted for that choice?"

Rolf ignored him. He said, quietly, "Heath, my dear, I am sorry about this — but it may be our only chance to help Donald. Do you mind answering one or two questions?"

"No, Oom."

"I am pleased. Now, listen: You told me last time I was here that Arthur Cooper is your half–brother?"

"Yes."

"You share the same name, and so it would be natural to assume that you share the same father. But my theory is that the connecting link between you is your mother. I say that your mother was married twice, that Arthur was the son of the first husband, and that he used his stepfather's name when your mother remarried. Am I right or wrong, Heath?"

"Right, Oom."

"Then Heath, do you know the name of your mother's first husband, Arthur's father?"

"Yes."

"And what was that name?"

"Prentice."

✪

The door closed on Johnson and his prisoner.

The boy still sat in lethargic fearfulness. Incongruously, a sobbing Heath ran to him for consolation. She put her arms around his shoulders and, barely perceptibly, he flinched. His eyes welcomed and sought escape.

Beresky and Rolf came to stand in front of him.

Beresky said: "Donald?"

"Yes?"

"You heard the talk in this room? You saw what happened?"

"Yes. But I don't... understand. This suspicion of Heath. I don't remember... "

"But you will, Donald, you will. There's just one thing for you to do. Fill your mind with it, Donald. Concentrate. Just on this one point: Heath is innocent. Say it."

"Proved innocent, Donald. You made a mistake. Just a mistake. And Heath is innocent. Your mind is full of that? Now try to remember."

The boy's muscles tensed. His head lolled. His lips twisted to form the word "innocent."

Beresky nodded to Rolf who suddenly and resonantly began to quote:

"Under hot Constantia broad the vineyards lie;
   Throned and thorned the aching berg props the speckless sky;
Slow below the Wynberg firs trails the tilted wain —
   Take the flower and turn the hour, and kiss your love again."

Beresky said: "Think!"

The boy bared his teeth, moaned, and moved his eyes in bafflement.

Rolf said, very slowly: "Take the flower. And turn the hour. And kiss your love again."

Winters' face shivered into a spasm. His muscles moved, twisted and sagged. Tears shot from his eyes.

"I remember now," he said.

❂

He came from the shop, dropping the old watch into his left-hand trouser pocket, fitting the new one on his wrist. He adjusted it to the City Hall clock, and started to wind. The time was 10.55.

A vague cloud passed through his mind. He should have wound first, of course. Maybe a minute . . . He looked up again at City Hall, but something stopped the sweep of his eyes.

A hand. Clutching a balcony rail. But not just any hand. A hand with a strange little finger which stuck out at right angles as it gripped. The same hand that had reached out to bludgeon him. The hand that had been red with Clyde Parson's blood. No doubt about it — he now had the murderer.

The hand moved, turned, bringing the body to which it belonged out of the shadows, showing the face clearly in the shattering light.

Heath.

He felt his feet shuffling, walking away with him.

He walked to the top of Plein Street. And down again.

Heath.

He thought of her always as a flower, as a white flower, like the heath in the poem. White and pure. White as sands of Muizenberg. With white hands. But they had once been red — wet with Clyde's own blood.

He had not sworn an oath — nothing so melodramatic as that. All the same there had been the *feeling* that if he ever found the murderer...

He had noticed the poster as he passed the first time, and now it seemed to bore into his brain with a new meaning, *Kiss the Blood off My Hands*. Kiss the blood off Heath's hands...

He crossed the road with long strides, and bought a ticket from the hard-faced blonde in the box. But somehow the poster drew him. He went to it, peered at the strip pasted across the bottom, and stiffened.

Crime Does Not Pay.

No escape. There it was again.

He wandered, and did not know he was wandering.

He thought of the new watch, and how he had felt about it symbolising a new life. He stripped the watch off his wrist, and took the old one out of his pocket. And then he saw the lilies.

The poem came back to him. Buy my heath and lilies. And here were lilies.

He looked at them, and then again the poem came: take the flower.

He took one. It lay in his right palm, a symbol of purity. And then suddenly the curves of the bloom reminded him of a hand, a white hand, with a strange little finger.

He crushed it.

And became conscious of the watches he held. Old life, new life.

He dropped the new life in the gutter.

But the poem persisted. Take the flower, and turn the hour and kiss your love again.

Kiss your love with the bloodstained hands.

Back, back, back. Back again to where it happened, here on the corner of Plein Street. Only she had gone. There is no hand on the balcony rail.

And turn the hour.

If only he could. Back again to 10.55. And the rest be a dream, yes, that would be a solution. Back to 10.55. And no hand on the balcony rail. No hand to meet his eye as it climbed to the City Hall tower, no hand because the hand was a dream, and the clock would now show 10.55. The clock *will* show 10.55...

The clock showed 11.47. And his watch. But... ?

The old watch, of course. A mistake.

He put his hand in his pocket, and pulled out an unused cinema ticket and a crushed white flower.

He had never seen them before.

THE ANGEL OF DEATH

This is, above everything else, an atmosphere story. Fog and vague figures swirling in the ambience of dim lights, coupled with strange sounds and noises are reminiscent to the average reader of Victorian London, the East End, cobbles, horse–drawn traffic and dark alleys. Even when you know the site is Cape Town docks something of a Jack the Ripper Menace still lurks. One asset here, though — the vital clue should be easy to solve by anyone who enjoys cryptic crosswords.

It was cold with an after–midnight clamminess, and only occasionally did the gaseous sponge of the mist swirl aside to let a tired star or two catch a momentary glimpse of the water in the Cape Town docks. Over on Mouille Point the lost cow of the foghorn mooed forlornly. On the East Pier, the black bulk that was the Smetterman had somehow turned itself into the shadow of a shadow, and the water sighed and the moorings groaned, and these noises were echoes of echoes.

Elias Mafuta, the dock guard crouched, almost embracing his brazier, and it was not alone the cold that made him shiver.

On the deck of the Smetterman there were movements where none should have been. There were two figures, one creeping, the other waiting, and death hovered...

The mist took the sound of the shot, wrapped it invisibly in grey cottonwool, and tried to smother it among the other night noises, but Elias heard. He drew another big shiver around himself like a blanket, because he was reluctant to break his not–sleeping concentration on the glowing coals, and besides he was afraid. He shook himself to a new alertness. This was a good job; he had better go and see. He turned up the wick of his hurricane lamp, gripped his knobkierie and shuffled forward. The heat of the brazier prickled across his legs and the cold air thrust at his face and his chest with moist fingers, but he went on. On and up the rickety gang–plank to the deck, holding his lantern out, peering around.

Some of the blackness detached itself, sprang at him, beat him to the boards with a jarring, raking impact of metal on his face, and then steps raced down the gangplank.

Elias scrabbled to his knees, groped in his pocket for his whistle, and sent blast after blast of sharp sound piercing the reluctant air. With grim satisfaction he visualised the men on duty at the dock gates hearing the whistle, stopping anyone from leaving the dock area until other instructions came. No, whatever had hit him would not get out of the docks tonight — not even if it was Tokoloshe himself.

He staggered to the lamp, which had rolled out of his hand into the scuppers, and turned to look for his stick. From the pier someone called: "Where are you, Elias? Was that your whistle?"

It was the guard from No.7 Quay, and Elias knew him.

"Yes, it is me," he called back. "I am on this ship. Hurry now to the Port Offices and fetch the harbour police and bring them here. Bad things have been happening."

"Bad things? What bad things?"

"There was someone on this ship, and when I came up I was struck so my head is bleeding, and now I find there is a white baas here, and he is dead. Do not waste time with questions — run for the police."

"The police are already coming, Elias. Listen. That is their putt–putt boat on the basin."

"Then call out to them, mompara, so that they may know from where the whistle came."

In answer to the shouts, the police launch came up alongside the Smetterman, and a half–dozen uniformed figures, with powerful electric torches, swung up the gangplank.

Elias was waiting to tell his story. They listened patiently, putting a question or two to keep him from becoming over–loquacious, then turned their attention to the man lying on the deck. That he was dead they had seen from the first flash of their torches. He had been shot at close range with a large–calibre bullet.

They searched the body to find traces of identity. The constable who felt in the breast pocket came out with a wallet and in it he found a card. He flashed his torch on it and whistled, and handed it with an exclamation to the sergeant in charge.

They left two men on the Smetterman, and the rest went by launch to the Port Offices. The sergeant used the telephone.

❂

Detective–Inspector Joubert, of the Cape Town C.I.D was not unused to having his beauty–sleep disturbed, but on this occasion he was both annoyed and sarcastic.

"So you found a body on a ship," he said. "So what? It's in the harbour area, isn't it? And that's completely out of my jurisdiction, or haven't the Railways and Harbours police got round to telling their sergeants that yet? As far as I know, that regulation has only been in existence since 1910... "

The sergeant was imperturbable. "It's not that, sir, I just thought that in the peculiar circumstances you would appreciate the opportunity to co–operate with us. In any event, we'd have to approach you for information later."

"Peculiar circumstances? What do you mean?"

"When we searched the body, sir, for purposes of identification, we found a warrant card which indicates the deceased was Detective–Constable Kelder of your department."

"Kelder! Good Lord! Thanks, sergeant, I'll be up as quick as I can. Oh, wait a minute — I take it you've sealed off the area? Good. Who'll be in charge of things your end?"

"Head–Constable Opperman, sir. He suggested I should phone you."

"Tell him thanks, Sergeant. I'll be bringing a couple of my men along, too. Goodbye."

"Goodbye, sir."

Now it was Joubert's turn to telephone. He got a grumbling Detective–Sergeant Johnson on the wire, explained the position briefly, and arranged a rendezvous. Then he dressed rapidly, climbed into his car, and made off. After a few blocks he stopped the car, reversed so that he could turn a corner and eventually pulled up at a large boarding–house. He went round the side and rapped on the window.

Almost immediately a light went on, and the hirsute face of Rolf le Roux peered at him reprovingly.

"Something might interest you," explained Joubert. "One of my men has been murdered on a boat in the docks. You can come with me if you like, but don't be long."

"I will come with you," said Rolf, "not because I want to, but because at my age when a man is woken up, he cannot sleep again. Wait for me in the car."

Despite his casualness, he was sitting at Joubert's side in a remarkably short space of time.

❂

"Come in, come in," said Opperman cheerfully, and motioned to the steaming mugs on his desk. "Have some coffee — although you don't really deserve it. If you're going to have your men murdered, I wish you'd have it done at Caledon Square instead of bringing them down here to the docks. What was the man doing here, anyway?"

While they were shaking hands, Joubert said: "Tell him, Johnson."

"Kelder was supposed to be on duty tonight," said Johnson. "I'd give a lot to know myself what he was doing here. On top of it, his job was specific. He was giving protection to a Durban man called Bingle, who is staying at the Pearl Hotel."

The last words were lost as a sudden gust of wind threw a hissing shower of rain at the window. He repeated them.

"Perhaps he followed Bingle here?" suggested Opperman.

"Not on your life. If he had, he'd have handed over to one of your men at the dock gates, or at least have reported himself, and I take it from what I've heard that he did neither. In any case, Bingle was so dead scared when he came to see us about protection, that I'm darned sure that the only thing that would get him out of his hotel room after dark would be a man–eating tiger under his bed."

"This Bingle now — what was he afraid of?"

Joubert answered this time. "He didn't give us any reasons — just told us that his life was being threatened. From what I gathered, it was in connection with some business transaction in Durban. He'd floated a company which went bung, and someone had started sending him anonymous letters, which put the wind up him. He didn't know himself, whether it was one of the shareholders or even one of the trade creditors — all he knew was that someone was after his hide, and I assure you he didn't like it."

"And Kelder?" asked Opperman. "Is he the sort of chap who'd neglect his duty if he thought he wouldn't be found out?"

"Definitely not," said Johnson. "Kelder was a nice chap — ambitious — and rather a serious type. I can't imagine any circum— stances which would make him neglect his work."

Joubert said: "It would have to be a darned strong motive to get him to leave a warm hotel for this." The gesture with his eyes pointed outside, where the fog and the cold waited like patient ghouls for the light and the warmth to die.

"And yet he came here," said Rolf. "Perhaps, after all, Bingle did go out, and he followed him. Why not telephone the Pearl Hotel and make sure?"

Opperman thumbed through the telephone book, held it open at the right page with one hand, while he clumsily dialed his number with the other. He spoke several seconds before he hung up. "That was the night porter," he said. "He knows Bingle well, and he is certain he has not left the hotel this evening. I told him not to worry about waking him at the moment."

"What about your side of it?" asked Joubert. "Did any of your men notice Kelder coming here?"

"Well, the chap on duty at the Kingsway entrance says someone who might have been Kelder came here about quarter to eleven. He seemed in a hurry and he looked at his watch as though he had an appointment to keep."

"And this same man didn't go out by any other gate?"

"Nobody answering to that description," said Opperman, a little grimly, "and nobody at all has left since almost the moment of the murder. The dock guard gave the alarm quickly, and the whole dock area was sealed off in a matter of minutes, I have a squad of men now rounding up the suspects. The murderer must be among them."

Rolf said suddenly: "The pockets," and then as the others looked at him, he explained: "It was probably Kelder who was seen at the dock gates, and he gave the impression that he was going to keep an appointment. If so, he may have had a note — "

Opperman opened a drawer. "This is what we found on him," he said.

There were five objects — a handkerchief, a bunch of keys, a fountain pen, propelling pencil, and a wallet. Rolf picked up the latter and looked through it. Kelder's warrant card was there, one or two personal papers, a banknote and several stamps. In the last compartment, Rolf's exploring finger pulled out an oblong newspaper cutting. "What have we here?" he said.

"Only a crossword puzzle," said Johnson. "Here, let's have a look at it. Yes. It's from yesterday's newspaper, Kelder was always doing the things. Darned good at it, too. I could only get out about four words in this one, and yet he's finished the thing off."

"And do you also," asked Rolf, "usually carry a puzzle around with you after you have finished it?"

"Not me — I chuck it away. But Kelder may have collected them for all I know."

"Even so," said Rolf, "I would like to look closer at this puzzle. Perhaps there may be something in it that he used as a reminder, which may help us."

"Go ahead," said Joubert. "I don't see that we can do anything more until the suspects are rounded up."

❂

Rolf and Johnson pored over the puzzle together. The rain paused for a moment, letting in other night noises, echoes, like the faint keening of an ambulance.

"You will notice," said the old man, "that he did not work out this puzzle easily. See, he had done the whole thing in pencil, and had only one word to get out — No. 7 down. He checked up on all his reasoning, filling over the pencil with a pen. And then, finally, at a later stage, he worked out 7 down, and entered the missing letters in pencil again."

"And what was this 7 down?" asked Joubert.

"The clue," said Johnson, " is A.B.s go on them. Clue number CC, and the answer is seven seas. Wait, I don't get that. Oh, yes, I do. A.B.s are sailors — sailors go on them. Right. Clue number? Of course — seven. And CC represents seas — a pun on the letters, seven seas. That's darned good — I'd never have worked out the solution from the clue alone. There's nothing particularly suspicious in that clue though, is there, Oom Rolf?"

"Not at first sight. But we haven't finished yet. What about these scratched out notes in the margin?"

"Let's see. Yes. That's how his mind worked around this 7 down. Look. He's tried to think out possible anagrams. The first one scratched out is the words TWO HUNDRED, which he thought

might have been the interpretation of the double C, considering it a
Roman numeral. Then he thought of CENTIMETRE in the same
connection, and scratched it out, too. And then he put down
ABTHEMCC — AB on THEM followed by CC. Also no good. He
followed this with ABSHIPCC, the ship being what A.B.s go on. And
finally he thought out the correct solution."

"What about those other notes?" asked Rolf. "You will see they
have been written much more firmly, as though he knew the
meaning and was not speculating. Look. LLA, heavily underlined,
and then underneath 11 to 18."

"I can't see where LLA fits into the crossword at all," said
Johnson, but what about the number? 18 — 18 — there's no 18
across, but 18 down is NIGHT. That's it. That's your appointment
— 11 to 18 — 11 tonight. That fits in with the time he was observed
at the dock gates."

Joubert and Opperman came around to see.

"So it was an appointment," said Joubert. "Still, I don't see that
helps much at this stage."

"Wait," said Rolf, and then to Johnson: "As far as I can see, these
crossword puzzle clues seem full of double meaning?"

"Yes."

"Then why must we assume that the only meaning of the clue is
eleven o'clock tonight? What about the figure 11 too? Perhaps
number 11 in the puzzle also has significance?"

"Eleven down," said Johnson, "AMERICANS. Possible. He may
have been meeting some Americans at 11 last night. Eleven across
— AZRAEL. That's some sort of angel, isn't it?"

Joubert said grimly: "The Angel of Death."

✪

The last syllable hung in the air, and then suddenly fluttered in
fear behind the foghorn. They looked at one another.

"It sounds prophetic," said Opperman, "Coincidence, of course,
but it is rather queer. It is almost as though he knew he was going
to be murdered."

"No," said Rolf. "You are wrong. Don't look at the solution —
look at the clue. The angel you have to meet, now we know the sex
of the person he had to meet — a woman whom he thought of as an

angel, whom he had to meet at 11 o'clock last night."

"Isn't that a bit far–fetched?" asked Opperman. "Why shouldn't it be the Americans he was meeting?"

"No, Johnson has told you Kelder was young and conscientious. Such a man would not leave his duty to meet all the Americans in New York City, whatever the incentive. But ever since the days of Adam, upright men have neglected their obligations because of women. Yes, the angel Kelder had to meet tonight was a woman — and her initials are LLA."

"We should be able to narrow down the search," said Joubert. "That's much more cheerful."

But Rolf was still sombre. He shook his head. "I do not like it," he said. "A large–calibre revolver is not a woman's weapon. I think he met the woman, because otherwise he would not have stayed so long on such a night, but a man fired the shot. Perhaps there was another reason for the appointment. Perhaps someone wanted Kelder out of the way."

Opperman said: "You mean, someone might have wanted to get at Bingle?"

"Perhaps. But in any case, Bingle may have been watching his watcher. Perhaps he noticed something about Kelder that may help us."

Opperman stretched out his hand again to the instrument on his desk.

"Don't phone," said Joubert. "Johnson, you'd better take my car and go up there yourself. Be tactful — you don't want to wake up the whole hotel unless there really is an emergency. Give me a ring from there."

"I think I would like to go with Johnson," said Rolf.

✪

Bingle was asleep, and he was no longer afraid of his own safety. He was beyond fear, and from his sleep there could be no awakening. Although the powder–blackened hand–towels in the floor showed how a silencer had been improvised, it was surprising that no sound had been heard, because the wound in the gaping forehead showed the revolver must have been of large–calibre.

"I s– s– saw nothing," stuttered the white–faced night porter. "I don't know h– h– how it happened. And I was w– w– wide awake too."

They had their doubt about that point; he had been fast asleep when Johnson and Rolf had arrived.

More questions.

The man in the room next door who had heard a muffled shot at 11 p.m. Telephone calls. Joubert, Caledon Square, then Joubert again. The arrival of Detective–Sergeant Botha and a grumbling Doc McGregor. Then back into the car, with the mist and the rain, and gusts of wind panicking before the wings of the Angel.

"That ship," said Johnson. "The Smetterman — I've heard about it. It's a dead ship. It shouldn't be where it is now. It was sunk during the war, and lay at the bottom of the sea for two years before it was salvaged. Haunted, too, they say. One of the divers was hauled up to the salvage vessel raving mad, screaming about something he had seen in the wreck." He shivered. "Not the sort of place I would choose to meet a girl on a night like this."

"You forget," said Rolf, "it was probably the girl's idea, and the Smetterman was an ideal place just for the reasons you have mentioned. Nobody on board, easy to slip past the dock guard, a reputation for ghosts — what could be better? Besides, don't forget that Kelder was brought there to be killed."

"To be killed? I don't get that. It seems to be he was brought there to get him away from Bingle."

"And to get killed," said Rolf. "He must have known the girl he met, and through her the murderer could be easily traced. There was never any intention of letting Kelder tell about that appoint—ment."

"So what do you think happened tonight?"

"There is only one thing that could have happened. Kelder is lured to the Smetterman by this girl, this LLA, while her friend, probably a man, kills Bingle. Then the man follows to the docks, the girl makes an excuse to leave Kelder so she can meet her friend and show him exactly where Kelder is, and then the man fires his gun for the second time."

"And the man and the girl?"

"Are probably still in the docks. We will catch them. Kelder's note of her initials on the crossword puzzle will send them both to the gallows."

The car pulled up before the dock offices.

✪

The dragnet had hauled in a small but mixed bag. Had the weather been fine, there would no doubt have been more people looking sullen or frightened or indignant in Opperman's office, but as it was there was only the merchant seaman reeking of liquor, the bedraggled woman whose age still showed through the streaked layer upon layer of make–up, the youngster with the mop of black hair and the shifty eyes, and the fresh–looking young man and the girl.

The sorting–out began. A young constable singled out the painted woman and the sailor, and reported he had found them together under a tarpaulin on No.5 jetty.

"Names?"

"Edward Carrera," said the sailor. He explained that he was a member of the crew of a vessel docked in the Duncan basin.

The woman was not so accommodating. "My friends call me Lily," she said, in answer to the query, "but seeing as how you're no friend of mine, it's none of your business anyway."

"I want a name for my records," said Opperman, with threatening politeness. "Now are you going to give me one? Or would you rather tell the magistrate?"

"All right," said the woman. "You can put me down as Smith. No, on second thoughts, put me down as Mrs. Opperman, and when the Beak asks me what I was doing on the docks, I'll tell him I was looking for my bigamous husband, the Head Constable."

Opperman wrote down "Lily Smith," on the docket. He turned to the constable. "What were they doing under the tarpaulin?"

"Oh... ah... They... "

The constable was young, and he threw an agonised glance at the well–dressed girl, and back again at his Chief. He blushed.

"What do you think we were doing?" said the woman, Lily. "Picking strawberries?"

"All right," said Opperman. "Next."

The boy with the mop of hair and nervous eyes said sullenly: "Smith, James Smith."

Opperman said to Joubert: "Aren't they original? It's marvellous how many Smiths get picked up by the police."

"One big, handcuffed family," said Johnson.

Opperman asked the boy: "What were you doing at the docks?"

"Looking for a ship."

Joubert suddenly slapped himself on the thigh. "That's probably true. I recognise him now, Opperman. His name's Van Zender and he's wanted for a neat little stick—up robbery in Paarl yesterday afternoon. Where's your gun, Van Zender?"

"There never was a gun. I pulled a water pistol on the fellow, and he nearly passed out from fright. I chucked it away in some bushes just a few yards down the road."

"And the money?"

The eyes grew still and bright with cunning. "You'd like to know, wouldn't you?"

Opperman said: "Lock him up." He turned his attention immediately to the young fellow and the girl. And what was in his attitude was reflected in the eyes of the others — the hard certainty that here stood the guilty pair — that what had passed before was duty, and therefore necessary, but the kernel of the matter had now been reached.

"My name is Sebastian," said the man, "Clement Sebastian, and I am a farmer from Hout Bay. My friend is Miss Chalmers, who stays at a hotel in Sea Point. Why are we being kept here?"

Johnson whispered in Rolfs ear: "Wrong initials," and the old man shook his head as though his vision was clouded.

Opperman had evidently the same idea. "Have you anything on you to prove your identity?" he asked.

Sebastian produced letters and a driving licence; the only document his companion could find was a hotel account addressed to Miss E. Chalmers.

"Do you know anyone with the initials LLA?" Joubert shot at them suddenly.

They pondered, then both answered, "No."

Sebastian repeated: "Why are we being held? What is all the trouble about?"

"A man was murdered here tonight," said Opperman, "and another man was murdered in the City. The same person is guilty of both crimes. Because you were in the dock area at the relevant time, you are under suspicion."

Sebastian laughed: "Why us? Do we look the type who'd go

around shooting people?"

Opperman pounced: "Who said anything about shooting?"

"Nobody."

After a slight wariness Sebastian was completely self–possessed. He motioned to Joubert. "This gentleman said something to the youngster about a pistol, and I simply put two and two together, that's all."

There was that in his attitude that made Joubert's hackles rise. "You don't look the type who makes a practice of sitting out in a storm either," he said. "What were you doing in the docks?"

It was the girl who answered.

"We came here, because we wanted to be alone. For a very special reason. We've just... got engaged tonight."

"Really?" There was enough sarcasm in Joubert's query to sting her.

"Yes, really. And you needn't take only my word for it. There's the constable who found us. Ask him."

"I must say," said the constable in question, "that when I flashed my torch into their car, they seemed well, very affectionate."

"Not to you, I'll bet," said Johnson, and the constable grinned.

Opperman said: "Do you know a Durban financier called Bingle?" and the answer was surprising.

"Of course I do," said Sebastian. "I had shares once in a company of his that went bust, so he can hardly be called a friend of mine. In addition I had some personal matters against the man. But why do you ask?"

"Because Bingle was one of the men who was murdered tonight."

"Oh, I see. Well, that doesn't make any difference. In fact I'm pleased I mentioned it. You'd have found out some time that I dis— liked him, and it might have looked bad if I'd have kept silent."

Opperman showed his teeth. "So that is why you mentioned the matter?"

"No," Sebastian smiled almost sweetly. "I merely answered a question. I did not know Bingle was murdered until you told me so."

Joubert struck out in a new attack: "Have you got a revolver?"

"No."

"Have you fired a revolver lately?"

"No."

"Any sort of firearm?"

"No,"

"Well then, Mr Sebastian, we're going to test the truth of your statement. There is a very useful method of finding out whether or not a man has fired a gun recently."

Sebastian laughed. "I've read about it. The paraffin–wax test. Only you're wasting your time in my case."

"If the test is negative then I will apologise."

"No, don't misunderstand me. There will be a positive result — but you can't use it as evidence against me."

Joubert was a little flustered. "What do you mean?"

"The paraffin–wax test is designed to show the presence of gunpowder on the skin of the man tested. But what you tend to forget is this — it is not alone a test for gunpowder, but for any nitrate, of which gunpowder is only one. Remember I told you I am a farmer? It is very easy for me to prove that any day — every day — I handle artificial fertilizer, and that artificial fertilizer is also a nitrate compound. Of course your test will be positive — as positive as it would be worthless as evidence in a court of law,"

Joubert said: "You seem to have made a special study of all this," but he had shot his bolt, and he knew it.

"Criminology is a hobby of mine," said Sebastian, and then: "Look, are you or are you not going to charge us? If you are, then get it over with. If not, then I would like to take my fiancee home."

They looked at each other. Eventually Opperman said: "All right. Go home. But don't try and leave town, or you'll be sorry."

"Come, Elsa," said Sebastian.

They had just reached the door, when Rolf stood up in excite—ment. "No," he said, "wait. They are guilty those two. I can prove it."

Joubert asked: "How?"

"The crossword puzzle in Joubert's pocket. Look. Here it is. Remember the word he found so difficult — 7 down? Seven Seas was the answer, and how was it worked out? By a pun. Look at the second part of the Clue: Clue number CC. The clue number was seven and the CC — the use of the letter C repeated — to provide a pun. C's – seas."

"We've gone over that before," said Johnson. "How does it help us now?"

"Can't you see? Put yourself in Kelder's place. He is fascinated

with the use of a letter in the plural to form a pun. He is pleased he
has worked out the trick. And at the same time he is thinking of a
charming lady he is leaving his duty to meet. So he puts down the
time of appointment, but above it he writes her name. And he writes
it in the same form as the crossword clue, by duplicating letters to
form a word of similar sound. Look, LLA — two L's and an A — L's
—A – Elsa!"

There was a slight sound from Sebastian, a sort of incipient
snarl, and the next second he and the girl were outside the door,
wrapping themselves in fog, clattering themselves into nothingness.

Whistles shrilled. Three constables grabbed torches, ran out, and
Opperman ran with them, but he was back in a few seconds. "They
won't get away," he said. "The dock gates are still sealed."

"There are other ways of escape," said Rolf, significantly.

Outside, two shots were fired by the constables. The little group
in the office came to peer through the door. There was another shot,
and a second later the beam from a flashlight caught Sebastian. He
was standing at the very edge of the dock. At his feet was the
crumpled thing that had once been Elsa.

He looked around wildly, fiercely, and then he sprang sideways.
There was the dull sound of a splash.

Men shouted. More torches flashed, beams of light criss–crossed
the water. Eyes peered. They saw nothing but the oily swell feebly
trying to shake off the cobweb of the mist.

Ears pricked, listening. They heard only the lazy amorous slap
of water on the quayside, the light gurgle of pleasure and rejection.
Suddenly the moo of the lost cow sounded very clear and near...

TIME OUT OF MIND

This story has a number of firsts. It is my first time paradox plot; the first story of mine to be printed in Ellery Queen's Mystery Magazine; *and the tale that inaugurated a long–lasting correspondence between Ellery (Fred Dannay) and myself.*

I was proud of the tale because it seemed to me to be an Open Sesame at last to the top market I had always wanted to attain. Fred liked it for a variety of reasons, but he was mainly intrigued that such a "tough" yarn had first achieved the light of day in Milady, *a highly–polished South African women's magazine. Apparently, no U.S. equivalent publication would ever have dreamed of accepting it. All this, I claimed, was living proof of how much tougher South African women were than their American sisters!*

From the battery on Signal Hill the midday gun boomed. The dull sound mushroomed out in the still air, shivered and was gone. The little table clock in the dining room started to strike. In the lounge the old grandfather clock cleared his throat wheezingly, preparatory to coughing out his deep chimes.

Miss Brett shook her head regretfully. It was all wrong, of course — the time was really half past three. All the clocks would have to be altered. She sighed and rose,

The minutes crept by. In her room plump Mrs. Fenwick opened her curtains slightly, and gazed at the smartly–cut shoes on her sill. She reached out her hand to touch them, and then the temerity of her actions froze her muscles. She remained with her hand stretched out, eyes drinking in the symmetrical music of the shaped and fluted leather, her soul caressed into ecstacy by wave after wave of adoration.

She stood like this a very long time.

Upstairs, old Mrs. Calloran looked at the mark on the wall and made baby noises all the time while Nurse Villiers washed and dressed and fed her; she was much worse than usual today. The nurse thought something might have upset her, but of course it was no use asking. So she left Mrs. Calloran cooing to the wall, and went out to gather the others together for lunch.

She found Miss Kemp flat on her stomach in the garden, peering fiercely through a rhododendron bush. As Nurse Villiers approached she sprang up suddenly, put her fingers to her lips, and said "Hush!" She continued, quite conversationally: "I'm looking for a tall man with a fair moustache. I don't think you've met him, but he's my husband. The Jungle Queen kidnapped him but I shot her with an arrow this morning, and now he's disappeared again. I must find him soon, or else the municipality will prosecute him for the bad drainage."

"Yes, yes," said Nurse Villiers, soothingly. "Have you thought of the dining–room? He may have gone there for lunch. All the others are going, you know."

Miss Kemp went like a lamb.

Mrs. Perry was peering in through the window of Sister Henshaw's office. When she turned round to face Nurse Villiers, her eyes were full of tears. "Everyone is against me," she said.

"Oh, come now," said Nurse Villiers, "nobody here hates you — we're all your friends. You'll feel much better after lunch,"

"You're not telling the truth," said Mrs. Perry. "Oh, it's too cruel. You all lie to me. Even Sister Henshaw lies to me."

"Really?" said Nurse Villiers, good–humouredly. "What about?"

"The knitting needle I lost. You know I looked everywhere for it, and Sister said she hadn't seen it."

"Yes?"

"Well, look," said Mrs. Perry, pointing through the window. "She's had it all the time!"

Nurse Villiers looked.

Until she caught a grip of herself, she felt the blood rushing from her head. Almost automatically she consoled Mrs. Perry, and led her gently to the dining–room. She saw all her charges settled and beginning the meal.

Only then did she go to the telephone, and dialed a number frantically. For endless seconds she heard the t–r–r–ing, t–r–r–ing of the bell on the other phone, then there was a click as the receiver was lifted, and a familiar voice came over the wire.

"Oh, thank God, doctor," she said. "This is Nurse Villiers here. Can you come over right away? Sister Henshaw is dead. Murdered. Yes, doctor, –U–R– yes. No, it couldn't be anything else. Please come right away, doctor... please!"

She put the receiver back on the rest, not to end the conversation, but because even that little action helped to steady her.

❂

The house was in the upper fringes of Oranjezicht, on the slopes of Table Mountain, and was set in large grounds surrounded by a high paling fence. It was called "The Haven."

The Cape Town police came in two cars. In the larger was Dr. McGregor, the medical examiner, Detective–Sergeants Johnson and Botha, and a uniformed driver. Lieutenant Joubert drove from Caledon Square in his own little Austin, and Rolf le Roux came with him. Dr. Patterson, as he had promised over the telephone, was waiting for them outside the wrought–iron gates.

He knew McGregor, and the medical examiner introduced him to the others.

"I want to make a statement," said Patterson, "but before I do, I would first like you to view the body. There are certain things I should point out on the spot."

The time was then a quarter past two.

They went into the room, and the unseeing left eye of Sister Henshaw stared at them. From the right eye the end of a steel knitting needle projected.

"The cause of death," said Patterson, "is obvious. But I want you to take particular note of the weapon."

"Any chance of fingerprints?" asked Joubert, but Johnson shook his head.

"Very doubtful," he said. "The surface of the needle is too small. Even if we did find more than a smear, it certainly wouldn't embody enough points to make a positive identification."

McGregor was examining the body, testing muscle flexion, peering carefully at the trickle of blood on the right cheek. He met Joubert's enquiring gaze, and shrugged. "Not less than one, and not more than four hours ago," he said. "I cannot be more accurate until I cut her up. But there is one thing that is strange. There is face–powder on this blood–trickle — someone powdered the corpse after death."

"I'm glad you noticed that," said Patterson. "I never looked closely enough myself, but I was going to point out the make–up to

you. You see, Lieutenant, it's completely out of the ordinary. Sister
Henshaw never used lipstick or rouge — and you'll note that there's
plenty of both on her face now."

He added: "As far as the time of death is concerned, I think I
may be able to narrow it down for you."

"Yes?" said Joubert.

"Not now, Lieutenant — when I make my statement later. First,
there is just one more oddity I would like to point out to you. Her
shoes."

Joubert squinted down at the body. "I see what you mean —
she's not wearing any. But why is that particularly strange? After
all, she seems to have lain down on the sofa for a rest which turned
into a nap, and was probably attacked while asleep, judging from the
lack of signs of a struggle. It would have been natural for her to
remove her shoes before lying down."

"You're missing my point, Lieutenant. I happen to know she
always takes her shoes off when about to lie down. But where has
she put them? I've had a fairly good look round, and I can't see them
anywhere. To my mind they've been removed from the room,
probably by the murderer."

Joubert said: "That's interesting," then added: "I think we
should have a thorough search before jumping to conclusions,
Johnson, Botha — let's get down to it."

They did. They peered under furniture, opened drawers and
cupboards, probed every possible aperture. No shoes.

"It seems you may be right, doctor," said Joubert. "Well let's find
another room where we can take your statement."

Rolf le Roux said: "Just a minute, Dirk." He was standing near
the head of the couch, unlit pipe gripped between white teeth and
projecting beyond his bushy beard. His soft brown eyes were peering
intently at the body.

Joubert looked at him enquiringly.

Rolf took out his pipe to use as a pointer. "The matter of the
make—up has been raised," he said. "Dr. Patterson has not theorised
a reason why it was done, and I don't know whether what I have
observed has a bearing on his explanation. Nevertheless, come and
look at this. You've already seen that the face was powdered after
death. Now note that the eyebrows were pencilled before the powder
was put on the face. You can see that, because the powder is over

the eyebrow pencil marks. Note too that the rest of the make–up is also under the powder. In other words, each individual cosmetic was put on first before the face was powdered.

Joubert shrugged. "And all this means?"

"I don't know at this stage, Dirk — except that it must have some significance. Perhaps after we've heard all the statements, things may become clearer... "

They moved into the lounge, found seats, and made themselves comfortable. Botha rested his notebook on his knee. Patterson spoke up clearly and concisely, like a man used to marshaling his facts.

"I'd better start with my personal connection with this affair," he said. "In the first place 'The Haven' is a residential clinic for psychotics — in popular terms, a private lunatic asylum. It is — was — owned by myself and Sister Henshaw in partnership. We have one other trained nurse as assistant. This is Nurse Villiers. At 1.15 pm today — yes I'm sure of the time; I made a note of it — she telephoned me at my house with the news that Sister Henshaw had been murdered. I rushed over here, inspected the situation without touching anything, and telephoned you immediately."

Joubert interrupted: "So it was not you, but Nurse Villiers who discovered the body?"

"Yes."

"Where is she now?"

"Upstairs, Lieutenant, busy with her duties. As soon as you've finished with me, I'll relieve her, and send her to you. May I go on?"

"Of course."

"What I want to tell you may possibly save you a good deal of unnecessary work. I don't know much about normal police methods, but I'm convinced this is not a rational crime, and any inquiries along normal channels is bound to prove fruitless. For instance, if you were to ask me if Sister Henshaw had any enemies, I'd have to tell you that I don't think she had a single friend. She was super–efficient, domineering, stubborn and almost aggressively insulting to everyone she came across.

"I can speak from personal experience. I recently had an offer for this property, which I thought we should accept, but Sister Henshaw refused. That was her right, of course. If that had been all, I'd have had no rancour, but that wasn't enough for her. No, she continually brought the matter up, for the sole purpose, apparently, of sneering at me for what she called my gullibility. So you see, I've had an accentuation of all her worst traits piled on my head in the last three weeks — and I can speak with authority on the effect she had on the people who disliked her. The reaction was to avoid her at all costs — not to do her physical harm."

"You realise," said Joubert, "that you have just provided us with what might be construed as a possible motive for murder?"

"I'm perfectly conscious of that," said Patterson, and smiled. "I'm also conscious of the fact that you'd find similar motives for every other person who knew her. I have told you my opinion as a psychiatrist that this isn't a rational crime. No, although I can't name the killer, I know where she is at this moment."

Rolf asked: "She?" and Joubert said: "Where?" at exactly the same moment. Patterson answered both.

"Somewhere in this house," he said. "We have five patients here at the moment — all women — and I am morally certain that one or the other of them is guilty of this crime." He sighed a little wearily. "And I'm afraid, Lieutenant, that my science, which should be able to help you, at this stage is baffled. At the time of my original examination of these patients, I couldn't discern homicidal tendencies in any of them. If I had, the one concerned would never have been admitted here — we have no facilities for dealing with violent cases, nor have I noticed anything subsequently which could indicate a changing to violence, although there is no doubt something like that has occurred. But in whom? It could be any of them."

Joubert said: "I see." He paused, then added: "You said some—thing just now about narrowing down the time factor?"

"Yes... You will realise in an institution like this it's necessary to adhere to a rigid routine in order not to upset the patients. Everything goes by the clock. The day starts at 6.30, and various well–defined duties keep Sister Henshaw busy until 11.30. At that time sharp, she goes into her office to lie down and rest, rising at 1 pm for lunch, which is served to her in her office. She stays there until I arrive to discuss cases and treatment with her at 3 p.m. sharp... During the period she is in her office, it is a rigid rule that she should not be disturbed until lunch. Nurse Villiers tells me the body was discovered at approximately 12.50 pm, which means that the murder must have been committed within the 30 minutes preceding that time."

"And the various things you pointed out to us in connection with the body?"

"They may have significance in terms of the case–histories of the various patients — but perhaps I should deal with them after you have seen the patients themselves. Would you like to come round with me now? They are all in their rooms at this time, waiting my visit."

Joubert hesitated: "I think perhaps we had better interview Nurse Villiers first. Would you call her for us? I'll send her for you again as soon as we have finished the interview."

❂

Patterson left, and shortly after Nurse Villiers came into the room. She took the chair Joubert indicated. In answer to his questions, she told of the conversation with Mrs. Perry, and how she looked through the window,

"I understand," said Joubert, "that this was approximately at 10 minutes to one?"

"Yes."

"And I suppose it was quite a shock to you to see your employer murdered in so brutal a fashion?"

"Naturally."

"Did you go in and examine the body to make sure life was fully extinct?"

"It wasn't necessary, Lieutenant. I know death when I see it. There was no possibility of her being alive."

Joubert said: "I see," and then added almost negligently: "And, of course, you hated her, too."

She sat up very straight. "Naturally I hated her. She wasn't a very likable person, but I didn't murder her, if that's what you're insinuating. I don't like your tone of voice, Lieutenant. I don't know how you've learned that I quarreled frequently with her, but I wasn't the only one. And I don't think that fact in any way justifies your attitude that I am under suspicion."

"No?" said Joubert. "Well, perhaps you can enlighten me in another direction. You say that at 10 minutes to one you looked through the window, and recognised with a shock that Sister

Henshaw had been murdered. How is it then, that you didn't telephone Dr Patterson until 1.15?"

She was still tense. "I can see you've had no experience of mental institutions. The first rule we learn is that under no circumstances must patients be upset. I adhered to that rule. I took Mrs. Perry to the dining–room, saw all the others were settled and started to eat their lunch, and then I went to telephone. I suppose in a way I should have reported the matter immediately — but it is also my duty not to alarm the people I am looking after. If I did wrong, I'm sorry."

"But surely Mrs. Perry had already been upset?"

"No, I don't think so — at least not in the way you mean. I had the impression that she was preoccupied with the discovery of the missing knitting needle, and didn't realise the significance of its... position."

Joubert nodded to Johnson, who closed his notebook and replaced it in his pocket. They stood up. Nurse Villiers seemed surprised.

"Are you finished with me?" she asked.

"For the moment," said Joubert. "We would like you to fetch Dr. Patterson. Tell him we are ready to accompany him on his rounds. We would like you to come round with us, too."

"I always go with the doctor from patient to patient," said Nurse Villiers. "It's part of my duties." She left.

McGregor took the opportunity to excuse himself. "I'm not a psychiatrist," he said, "and I've got an autopsy to perform. If you dinna mind, I'll take the car, and then send it back to you. When the van arrives, show them where the cadaver is."

He waved farewell, not only to them, but also to Dr. Patterson and the nurse, who had just arrived.

"I'm going to follow my regular round, if you don't mind," said Patterson. "The first is Mrs. Perry, the owner of the weapon that killed Sister Henshaw. The clinical diagnosis of her case is paranoia — the insanity of delusions. She believes she is being persecuted. Like all the others here, she comes from a good family. Her insanity dates from the time her husband left her."

While he talked, he led them along a passage, eventually knocking on a door, which he pushed open without invitation.

Mrs. Perry looked up wild–eyed from the bed on which she was sitting. "Oh, doctor," she said. "It wasn't my fault. Really it wasn't my fault. I know everyone blames me but I didn't mean it."

"Didn't mean what, Mrs. Perry?"

"Letting the patient die under the operation, doctor. It wasn't my fault. The scalpel slipped, that was all."

"We know it wasn't your fault, Mrs. Perry. I hear you've got good news for me? I hear you found your knitting needle?"

Mrs. Perry became quite animated, but it was the animation of despair. "Oh no, doctor, I thought I had, but I hadn't. I know where it is, though. Sister Henshaw has it, and she won't give it up. She hates me. I know she hates me. She has a look in her eye... "

At a signal from Patterson, the police party backed out into the corridor. They heard Mrs. Perry sobbing, and a soothing undertone of words; eventually the doctor and nurse joined them.

"The next," said Patterson, "is Miss Brett. Quite frankly, there is no formal clinical word to describe her condition. She is perfectly normal, except for one irrational fixation. It appears that when she was a young girl her watch was wrong, and she missed an important appointment. I suspect it was probably a vital tryst with a lover. Ever since then, she spends her entire waking hours ascertaining the time, and checking its correctness. You may question her yourself, if you like."

He led them into a room, and introduced them to Miss Brett. Joubert saw her eyes travel to his wrist watch, and then to the clock on the dressing table. He felt almost relieved that the two instruments agreed.

"Do you remember what you did this morning, Miss Brett?" he asked her.

"Oh yes, I didn't waste a minute."

"Did you see Sister Henshaw go into her office?"

"Yes, that was at half past 11."

"Did you see anyone else go into her office?"

"No, that's impossible. I wasn't there, anyway. I went round to check the clocks."

"And did you return a little later?"

"Yes. Just before the noon gun went off. There was something wrong with it today, though. It went off at the wrong time. I had to alter every clock in the house. And then I had to alter them back. Because of lunch, you see. I wonder why it happened?"

Joubert said: "I'm sure I don't know." He had quite obviously thrown in the towel. He added: "Thank you," and "good afternoon," and sidled into retreat.

"I think you do much better than I do," he told Patterson. "I'll leave the others to you." He added: "In any case, little as I got out of her, I still have the impression that she's by no means a murderous type."

Patterson looked at Nurse Villiers, and smiled. "As a matter of fact, Lieutenant," he said, "Miss Brett is the only one of all our patients who has ever given an indication of violence. It happened the other afternoon. When we made our rounds, she was out of her room when we arrived — probably checking up on the clocks — and Sister Henshaw tactlessly asked her why she was late. Miss Brett became quite hysterical, and would certainly have assaulted Sister Henshaw if Nurse and I hadn't intervened."

He stopped outside a third door. "I'm afraid we're going to get very little out of this patient, Lieutenant. She is what is technically termed a foot fetishist — the only real emotional response she gives is to feet or footwear. I'm afraid it's not uncomplicated, either. There are definite symptoms of religious mania."

He turned the handle and walked in,

Mrs. Fenwick, coarse, crude and fat, knelt at the window with an expression of ethereal spirituality in her eyes. She was gazing at a pair of shoes on the sill. Her lips were moving, but without sound, and her hands were clasped under her chin. It was obvious that she was talking to the shoes; just before she rose, Joubert saw, with a quiver of shock, that she mouthed the word "Amen."

Patterson questioned her, but her answers were vague and meaningless, and she looked not at their eyes but their feet.

Nurse Villiers suddenly shivered, and caught Joubert by the arm. "The shoes on the sill," she said. "They're Sister Henshaw's. She was wearing them this morning."

Patterson heard her. "Tell me, Mrs. Fenwick," he said sharply, "where did you get those shoes by the window?"

For the first time she seemed to understand. "They came!" she said. "It was a miracle. They came with the pain of fire and the flash of steel! Let us pray."

She was down on her knees again, and Patterson shrugged. They moved out of the room.

They went upstairs.

Patterson asked Miss Kemp what she had been doing that morning, and she smiled knowingly. "I will tell the Court Martial," she said. "In the meantime, it's a secret. Only you and I know, eh Nurse?" She would say nothing more.

Outside the room, Nurse Villiers said: "She's very strange today. I mean more so than usual. I think I know what she was referring to about a secret, though. She told me this morning that she'd killed the Jungle Queen with an arrow. Oh, Doctor, do you think...?"

"Why her particularly?" said Patterson, and turned to Joubert. "As a matter of fact, Lieutenant, if I were to suspect one more than any other, on psychological grounds, I would choose Mrs. Calloran, the old lady we are now going to see. Let me explain. There is an insanity called dementia praecox in which the sufferer gradually regresses mentally to the behaviour of an infant. By the time the patient reaches the final stage, all cognitive power and initiative is lost, Mrs. Calloran has apparently regressed to the equivalent of a child of 10 months. However, I have come to the conclusion that she is not a typical praecox patient at all. For instance, it is only her emotional responses that have been affected — I am reasonably satisfied that she can act as purposefully as you or I, under certain conditions and circumstances. Remember the make–up on Sister Henshaw's face? Mrs. Calloran once owned a beauty parlour. Against this, of course, is the irrefutable fact that the door of her room is always kept locked."

He turned the key as he spoke, and opened the door.

Mrs. Calloran lay on her back on the bed, with a large wax doll gripped in her left hand. She was rolling from side to side, and crooning inarticulately. She stopped the movement suddenly, vindictively jabbed her extended forefinger in the doll's eye and said "Goo!"

She did not even look at them.

"It's no good talking to her in this state," said Patterson. "Let's go downstairs and finish our discussion."

In the lounge again, Joubert said: "Naturally, I have come to my own conclusions, doctor — but, after all, you are the expert. You said you would attempt to correlate the evidence found in the room and on the body with the case–histories of the various patients. Will you do so now?"

"Yes," said Patterson, and lit a cigarette. "I must stress again that although there are clues pointing in certain directions, they are not conclusive — in fact, they are mutually contradictory, and I can make very little sense out of them. I think the best thing for me to do is to run through the arguments for and against the guilt of each individual patient.

"First, Mrs. Perry. The weapon was a knitting needle which she made a great fuss of losing two weeks ago. She has a persecution mania, and often such a mania can become a homicidal drive. It is psychologically possible, if she found a needle in Sister Henshaw's possession, that she would attack her. On the other hand, her attitude that Sister Henshaw is still alive and still has the needle seems to argue against that possibility — and I can't find grounds, psychiatric or otherwise, which would have led her to remove the shoes or make the face up.

"The same objection holds good for Miss Brett and Miss Kemp, although we must have suspicions against the former for her violent attitude last week; and against the latter for her cryptic remarks to Nurse Villiers. The disappearance of the shoes and their recovery definitely seems to point to Mrs. Fenwick, but I can't imagine her committing such a crime, or in such a manner.

"The most likely psychological type, as I mentioned before, is Mrs. Calloran, and the making–up of the face seems to point in her direction. Even the method of the crime is quite consistent with her mentality — did you notice her gesture with the doll? — and, assuming we are correct in our suspicions that she is possibly a lot more mobile than she appears, she could have removed the shoes and placed them on Mrs. Fenwick's window sill. Only, of course, her door was locked."

"Are you quite sure?" asked Joubert, and turned to Nurse Villiers. "Isn't it possible, Nurse, that Mrs. Calloran's door was left unlocked for even a few minutes during the morning?"

She said, very positively: "No. I went into the room half a dozen times during the morning, and each time I both unlocked and locked the door. I was last there about a quarter to 12, when I changed her clothing and fed her. I distinctly remember locking the door when I left, because I had to put the tray on the floor to do so. I also remember unlocking it when I came in, for the same reason."

Patterson threw up his hands in a gesture of frustration. "There you have it, Lieutenant. That one of them did it, I am perfectly sure, but which one I cannot say. I don't even know whether the points I have brought up in defence are valid or not — they only represent my own opinion. If the various factors had made a consistent pattern, I would have had no hesitation in pointing to one or the other of the suspects. As it is... "

"But there is a consistent pattern," said Rolf le Roux, and the others turned to him in surprise. "Yes, doctor," he went on, "all your reasoning has been completely logical, except your conclusion. The individual clues point to one or the other of your patients; not all of the clues point to any one of them. Yet you have fallen into the fallacy of still contending that one of your patients is the guilty party."

"What is your interpretation?" said Patterson.

Rolf seemed to sheer off from the subject abruptly. "Before I go into details, there are one or two points I want to be perfectly clear about. First that the routine of this house is always unchanging?"

"Yes."

"That in accordance with this routine you never arrive until a quarter to three? In other words, at the time the murder was committed you were neither here, nor expected for some time?"

"Quite right."

"So that when Sister Henshaw went to lie down at 11.30, the only person about who had anything to do with the handling of patients, who knew about the routine, was Nurse Villiers?"

"Yes — but what are you getting at?"

"The only explanation of the clues. Yes, I'll tell you now. I say those clues were deliberately laid by the murderer, and that therefore the killer was a person with some knowledge of the mental twists of your patients. Contrary to your theory, the crime was perfectly rational and premeditated."

Nurse Villiers said: "You can't — " and then all eyes flicked towards her, but Rolf raised his voice smoothly to interrupt.

"The clues themselves," he said, "help us a little further in the matter. Remember the make—up on the face, and consider that in the light of the fact that the crime was a rational one."

Joubert said: "Explain, please."

"Remember how I pointed out the powder was over the pencilled eyebrows? There is a definite indication as to the sex of the murderer. Women use eyebrow pencil after the face has been powdered, not before. No, the murderer is a man."

The eyes swung back to Patterson. He stubbed out his cigarette violently. He said: "Do you realise the seriousness of your allegation? Do you think a theory, however ingenious, is sufficient evidence?"

"No," said Rolf, "but that can still be remedied." He turned to Nurse Villiers. "Bring Miss Brett in here."

There was no sound in the room until the nurse returned. Patterson lit another cigarette.

Rolf said to Miss Brett: "You told us before that you saw Sister Henshaw going into her office, and left to check the clocks?"

"Yes."

"What was the time?"

"It was half past 11."

"You mean, it was half past 11 because Sister Henshaw went into her office?"

"Of course. It's always half past 11 when she goes into her office."

"And if the clocks showed a different time, then you would put them right?"

"Naturally."

"You remember when the gun was fired on Signal Hill this morning? You told us something was wrong with it, and you had to alter all the clocks. What was wrong with the gun?"

"Usually when it fires it's 12 o'clock. Today it was half past three."

Rolf leaned forward in his chair. His voice was calm, but his knuckles showed white from the pressure of his fingers round his pipe.

"You mean," he said, "that as the gun fired today, something else happened which always happens at half past three?"

"Of course. What else could I have meant?"

Rolf sat back, relaxed. His voice was very quiet. "Tell me, Miss Brett, how do you know when it is half past three? What happens every day which tells you it is half past three?

"Don't you know?" she asked in surprise, and then added as though instructing a child: "It is half past three every day when Dr. Patterson comes out of Sister Henshaw's office."

THE FACE OF THE SPHINX

*Sphinx, n. Figure of crouching lion with woman's head. Enigmatic person. (Gk.)
— Oxford English Dictionary. That's all the reader needs to know at the moment. When
the reading is over, a footnote will explain why this tale is unique.*

The first news of the skolly with the mole on his face and his even
more fearful canine companion was carried in sensational fashion on
the front page of the *Cape Mail*. Readers who, that morning, bought
the paper and casually glanced at it to see what was new in South
Africa and the world had their attention immediately transfixed by
the bold headlines and the article which followed:

GEMS FOR ROYAL NECKLACE STOLEN
BRUTAL ATTACK ON DIAMOND MERCHANT AND
SECRETARY

"Six perfectly matched and flawless polished diamonds which
were to have formed part of a presentation necklace to the Queen of
England have been stolen in a daring Cape Town raid.

"The jewels, together with a number of lesser gems and £2,420 in
cash to a total estimated value of £800,000 were taken from an office
safe in Buitengracht Street.

"The raid began at 6 p.m. yesterday with a knock on the door as
diamond merchant Mr. J.M. Breel of 804 Buitengracht Street and
Miss M. Cornelius, his secretary, were finishing off the day's work.

"Miss Cornelius called 'come in', but there was no reply. A few
seconds later there was another knock on the door, and she opened
it.

"She was immediately overwhelmed by a Coloured man who
clapped one hand over her mouth and with the other brandished the
sharp point of a knife at her throat.

"At the same moment, a large tawny mongrel dog shot past them
into the office, sprang at Mr. Breel, knocked him over and stood with

98

snarling jaws a bare inch from his jugular vein.

"The skolly then forced Miss Cornelius back into the office and shut the door. The safe had already been closed but the keys were still in the lock. Holding the knife in his left hand, the raider opened the safe and removed the gems and a bundle of notes which were in a small drawer which contained a quantity of uncut diamonds.

"Warning Miss Cornelius that if she made a sound the dog would 'tear the man's throat out,' the man backed out of the office, leaving the door open. A few seconds later there was the sound of a whistle from the street, and the dog left Mr. Breel and shot down the stairs.

"While Miss Cornelius telephoned the police, Mr. Breel ran down to see if he could follow the assailant. By the time he reached the street, however, there was no sign of either the man or the dog.

MARK ON THROAT

"Miss Cornelius who showed the Cape Mail reporter a cut on her throat caused by the pressure of the knife, did not think there was any possibility of securing fingerprints, since the skolly had been wearing cotton gloves. However, she was certain that both she and Mr. Breel would be able to identify the man.

" 'I would know him anywhere,' she said. 'In fact, I am afraid I'm going to have nightmares of that face for a long time to come.'

"The police have issued the following official description of the wanted man: Height 5 ft 10 or 11 inches; weight, approximately 170 lbs.; complexion, light coloured; colour of eyes, brown; black hair grown long and parted on the right–hand side; small ears; medium straight nose; thin lips; large mole on right of forehead, approximately the shape of South America; wearing brown jacket and shoes, khaki trousers; probably accompanied by brown, long–tailed mongrel, approximately three feet high.

REWARD OFFERED

"Mr. Breel has authorised the *Cape Mail* to announce that he is willing to pay the sum of £2000 reward to any person supplying information leading to the arrest and conviction of the wanted man.

" 'Although the diamonds were covered by insurance,' he said, 'the gems for the Queen's necklace are perfect specimens and are probably irreplaceable. I feel it is my duty to offer this reward because the audacity and brutality of the criminal, show him to be a real menace to society.'

"Detective–Sergeant Johnson said that although the criminal apparently escaped without leaving a clue, the police were following up certain lines of investigation and he confidently expected the guilty man to be apprehended at an early date."

The *Cape Planet* carried a new sensation. The theft of the Queen's diamonds, it contended, was but one of a series of brutal crimes that could be laid at the door of the skolly with the mole.

"On the evening of Saturday before last," said the relevant article, "Mr. J. Bingham was alone in his house in Comoy Avenue, Rondebosch, his wife and daughter having left earlier by car for a cinema in Cape Town.

"Mr. Bingham was writing a letter at his dining–room table, when he heard a noise at the open window. He looked up, but before he could make a move a large brown dog sprang at him, knocked him to the floor, and stood snarling with its teeth at his throat.

"Realising the slightest move would cause the animal to snap, Mr. Bingham lay still.

"A Coloured man, carrying a knife and wearing blue–grey gloves, and whose description tallies in every way with that of the man sought for the diamond robbery, climbed through the window into the room. Without speaking, he went into the interior of the house and could be heard moving around. Later he returned and searched Mr. Bingham's pockets, removing a watch, a wallet containing £70 in notes and some silver.

"He then left through the window and a few minutes later the dog followed him in answer to a whistle down the road.

"The police were immediately called and it was discovered that in addition to the goods taken from Mr. Bingham, several small pieces of jewellery belonging to his wife and a wrist watch of his daughter's had also disappeared.

"In his description given to police at the time, Mr. Bingham made particular reference to the mole shaped like a map of South America on the right of his assailant's forehead.

"Two days later a similar ordeal was undergone by Mrs. J. Murdoch of Bellville, who was in Sea Point on holiday at the time.

"She left her boarding house at 2 p.m. and travelled by bus to

Kloof Nek, where she began a walk through the Glen intending to reach Clifton from where she would take a bus home.

"A short distance past the Round House she noticed a large brown dog and called to it. The animal seemed friendly enough, and approached her. When two or three yards away, however, apparently in response to a low whistle, it sprang at her, knocked her to the ground and threatened her throat with its teeth,

"At the same time a Coloured man emerged from the bushes, grabbed her handbag and disappeared the way he had come. A few seconds later the dog left her and also bounded into the bushes out of sight.

"Although Mrs. Murdoch had only a momentary glimpse of her assailant, there can be no doubt it was the same criminal as in the other cases. She, too, noticed the characteristic mole on the forehead, and she was struck by the fact that he was wearing cotton gloves.

"The robbery was reported to the police at Camps Bay. Although there was only a few shillings in the bag, Mrs. Murdoch suffered the loss of personal and business papers and an opal brooch of sentimental value."

Panic is a peculiar infection. The publication of the three cases together would probably only have evoked mere interest in the average reader had all the crimes been committed in a well defined area. But the outrages were scattered — Rondebosch, the centre of the City, the Camps Bay side of the Glen — so that there arose a feeling of disconnection. Men and women throughout the Peninsula all had the same thought: "He might strike here next."

And so that night those indoors carefully locked all entrances, and came back again and again to make sure they had forgotten no possible fastening. Outside, men looked over their shoulders frequently, and jumped at commonplace night noises.

The cold breath of fear had come over the mountain with the South–Easter, but it did not blow out to sea. It lay like an invisible fog over the bright green of the Peninsula.

In the morning, the tension of panic, unrelieved by physical action, found its outlet in indignation.

The *Cape Mail* leader, like that in the *Cape Planet* the same evening, called for the reinforcement of the South African Police in Cape Town, and the cleaning up of the Cape Coloured area of District Six.

That night a fight between Europeans and Coloureds started in Hanover Street. The initial cause of the uproar seems to have been an attack by three European youths on a Coloured man walking with a dog. Whatever the cause, the results were serious. When the police arrived, they found two Coloured women unconscious on the sidewalk. The European youths had disappeared.

It was not long before they were discovered. At 9.15 p.m. Police–Constable Claassen and Sergeant Faure, patrolling the maze of narrow streets and alleys near the main thoroughfare, came across the missing young men trussed together in a gutter. Two of the youths had evidently been bludgeoned into insensibility; the third showed no signs of having been beaten up, but both ears had been neatly sliced off.

A blast on the police whistle brought reinforcements and the youths were carried to Castle Bridge to await the arrival of the ambulance, There a considerable crowd gathered and, as the details of the outrage became known, something like insanity spread.

Groups of Europeans, shouting slogans and imprecations, broke away from the muttering mob, looking for Coloureds on whom to take revenge. An innocuous–looking Malay boy on a cycle on the Woodstock main road was attacked and knocked unconscious in a few seconds; on the other side of the crowd, 60 or 70 Europeans chased a horde of shrieking non–Whites up Hanover Street, striking unmercifully at those within reach.

The bloodlust had taken command, and for a moment the police were powerless. In fact it was well past midnight before the last group had been dispersed, and only at 6 a.m. did the ambulances cease their non–stop commutations between the hospitals and District Six.

At 1.30 a.m a well–dressed Coloured man entered the office of the *Cape Mail*, handed in an envelope marked Urgent News, and left before anyone thought of interrogating him. The contents caused the Night Editor to rearrange for the fifth time the layout of the front page splash of this modern St. Bartholomew's Eve. He made provision for a heavy box in the centre of the page, with a sensational headline, a brief intro and the text of the letter as follows:

"We, the Circle Gang and the Aces, being the largest two gangs in District Six, hereby declare that in view of the wholesale attacks on the Coloured people tonight we have decided to sink our differences and operate as one united organisation against the common menace.

"We hereby issue warning that we have instructed our members to KILL ON SIGHT any group of two or more Europeans found within the area of District Six between sunset and dawn.

"This order does not apply to members of the South African Police who, we believe, honestly tried to protect our people."

✪

Dawn saw the early morning haze over Table Mountain — but that was all that was usual about the city. Business men and their employees, coming into town by car, train and bus, were oppressed by a strange sense of desolation, despite the numbers of people and traffic about. It was only later they realised the source of the feeling — there was not a Non–White face to be seen in the central city area.

This, and the news in the *Mail,* caused uneasy glances to be cast in the direction of District Six. The Coloured areas, too, were watching the centre of the city. Over Cape Town lay a blanket of wary tension, as though each group was waiting for the other to make a move.

In his office at Caledon Square a red–eyed and weary Lieutenant Joubert looked almost with resentment as Rolf le Roux entered, showed his white teeth between moustache and beard in a cheery smile, sat down and filled his cherrywood kromsteel with strong Boer tobacco.

Detective–Sergeant Johnson was there, still not too tired to be facetious, Sergeant Botha and a half a dozen others.

"We must face this thing squarely," said Joubert. "It is possible nothing further will happen, but I am afraid the slightest incident will precipitate a first–class race riot. This whole business arises from the theft of the diamonds from Breel. If we can arrest this skolly with the mole on his face, the agitation will die down. How far have you got, Johnson?"

"Nowhere, Dirk. This trick of the dog keeping things quiet while he gets a good start has worked only too well. However, I sent out this morning to round up a couple of the leading gangsters in the hope they may tell us something,"

"Who has been brought in?"

"Duck and Telephone. Would you like to interview them now?"

"Yes."

One of the constables went out and returned with two Coloured men. Even if they had not been so well known, it would have been obvious at first sight which was which. Duck, one of the higher–ups of the Circles, had a low, broad forehead, a flat nose and projecting lips. He was comparatively rotund, and his feet facing outward made him waddle in a striking likeness to the bird after which he was named. His total appearance was deceptively respectable; he was in "civilian" life, a solicitor's clerk.

On the other hand, his companion, one of the leaders of the Aces, could never be mistaken for anything but a skolly. His round, flat face, tall, thin body, and enormous feet gave the clue to the origin of his nickname. On this occasion it was obvious he had relegated himself to the position of Duck's yes–man, no doubt in deference to the latter's legal background.

Joubert got down to business briskly. "What is the meaning of this notice," he asked, holding a *Cape Mail* in front of their noses.

Duck examined the article with an air of innocence. "It would seem," he said, "that the Aces and the Circles object to attacks on the Coloureds."

"Don't try to bluff me," said Joubert. "We know you well enough that you, Duck, control the Circles, and you, Telephone, are leader of the Aces. Why have you given this order to kill?"

"I gave no such order," said Duck blandly and "Me neither," echoed Telephone.

"Well, if you didn't, then who did?"

Duck hunched his shoulders in an obviously insincere gesture of innocence. "Perhaps it was a bow–tie," he suggested.

"I'm sure it was a bow–tie," said Telephone.

Joubert knew, and they knew he knew, of the implicit obedience given by every District Six gangster to any member of that secret society whose headquarters are in Pretoria Central Prison, and whose identifying mark is a tiny bow–tie tattooed on the throats of its members.

The conversation may have got no further, but —

"Did the Bow–tie who gave the order have a mole like the map of South America on his forehead?" asked Johnson.

Duck looked up sharply. "I know of no Bow–tie like that," he said.

"Do you know anyone of that description?"

"No," said Duck and Telephone also shook his head.

Joubert interrupted: "Look here, you know the man we mean — the one with the dog, the one who stole the diamonds. I don't know if you realise it, but the feeling against this man was the real cause of what happened last night. If you could help us find him, all the threat to your people will be removed. And the," he added with a grin, "you and Telephone could start fighting each other again to your heart's content."

Duck was thoughtful. "I know many men who make their living with their dogs at night," he said, "but none who look like this man. There is a great deal of truth in what you said about him causing the bad feeling, and I would like to see him caught.

"I'll tell you what, Lieutenant, I'll speak to my friends not to enforce that order for three days, and they will listen to me for that time provided they are not further provoked. If you can find the man you want by then, I do not think you will have further trouble,"

"I do not think so either," said Telephone.

When they had gone, Johnson said: "That sounded to me remarkably like an ultimatum."

"No," said Joubert, "I think it was a reprieve, and I think they meant what they said."

"But what is all this fuss about?" asked Rolf le Roux, and the others stared at him for several seconds before they grasped that he really was in ignorance of the situation.

"Don't you read the newspapers?" asked Johnson and gave him a brief account of events up till that time.

"I think I may be able to help you," said Rolf.

They turned to him, interested. "Have you seen this skolly somewhere?" asked Joubert.

"No. There is something in these reports... " He tapped the sheaf of newspaper clippings they had given him. "But I am not yet sure. Now, if I had the original statements made by these people... "

"Get them," said Joubert.

In a matter of seconds they were in the old man's hand, and he was studying them while the others watched. After a while he looked up again and there was a satisfied smile on his face.

"What have you found?" asked Joubert.

Rolf said: "The face of the Sphinx."

Joubert was irritated. "What do you mean?"

"Look, Dirk, we have here three distinct cases where the man has been described. Miss Cornelius and Breel have given the fullest details and from their statements and the corroboration of the others a picture of a face emerges. It is a cruel face, but a strong one — with black hair, brown eyes, straight nose, small ears, thin lips and, of course, a mole shaped like a map of South America."

Johnson said: "I see what you mean. If it wasn't for the mole the face would resemble that of the Egyptian Sphinx."

Rolf shook his head. "No," he said, "it was the mole particularly that made me think of the Sphinx." He puffed at his pipe, and went on: "Don't you see what a remarkable feature this mole is? Each of the four people who have seen it noticed it particularly and remarked on its peculiar shape. It is the one outstanding mark of identification we have for this skolly. That is why I spoke of the face of the Sphinx."

"You mean that despite the strong feature the face still remains inscrutable?" asked Johnson. "Are you implying that the mole was not a natural one — that the skolly used it as a form of disguise?"

Rolf shook his head, but Joubert interjected before he could speak. "Face like a Sphinx, mole like a map of South America — what difference does it make?" he asked irritably. "The point is, have you spotted anything that will help us find this man?"

"More," said Rolf. "I can save you all the trouble of looking for him. Let's make a bargain, Dirk — give me these dockets to take away with me, and then wait for my telephone call. I promise you that within an hour of that call your search will be over."

"I'm willing to try anything once," said Joubert. "Take the dockets. When will you be telephoning?"

"Some time between seven and eight tonight," said Rolf, and made a farewell gesture with his pipe as he passed through the doorway.

❃

If there had not been a general election pending, matters might indeed have ended as simply as that — a telephone call, a swoop by police, an article in the *Cape Mail* — and then even the sensations of the trial would have only had a vicarious interest to a public whose basic fears had been completely allayed.

But as the fact remains, as Rolf was pecking out on his portable typewriter the correspondence he knew would lead to the final denouement, a high–speed printing press was spewing out thousands of copies of a handbill whose effect could only be to complicate the position.

The handbill bore the underlined name of the political party which was paying the printing costs, and then continued:

WHITE CIVILISATION IS AT STAKE

Do you know:
- THAT THE SKOLLY WHO STOLE THE BREEL DIAMONDS AND SO BRUTALLY ASSAULTED OTHERS, INCLUDING WOMEN, IS STILL AT LARGE?
- THAT CRIMES OF VIOLENCE BY NON–EUROPEANS ARE ON THE INCREASE?
- THAT THE SKOLLIES OF DISTRICT SIX HAVE THREATENED TO KILL ON SIGHT ANY EUROPEAN THEY COME ACROSS?

THIS IS A DECLARATION OF WAR!
THE POLICE AND THE MILITARY WILL NOT ACT BECAUSE THEIR HANDS ARE TIED BY THE GOVERNMENT'S FATAL POLICY OF LIBERALISM TOWARDS THE NON–WHITES OF SOUTH AFRICA.
MEANWHILE OUR LIVES AND THE LIVES OF OUR WIVES AND CHILDREN ARE BEING THREATENED.
ARE YOU GOING TO SIT IDLY BY AND WATCH ALL YOU HOLD DEAR PLACED IN JEOPARDY?
NO!
Come to the
MASS PROTEST RALLY
on the
GRAND PARADE
at seven o'clock
TONIGHT

Arrangements for the distribution of this prize piece of political incendiarism were very thorough. Groups of youths carrying huge sacks of handbills swept through the town early in the afternoon, while almost simultaneously other groups began work in the suburbs. By five o'clock probably every European in the Cape Peninsula had had a handbill thrust into his hand, fastened to the windscreen wiper of his car, pushed under his locked door.

Very early in the afternoon, also, a copy of the handbill came into Joubert's possession, adding considerably to his worries. He called a conference, and thrashed the matter out. It was decided that it was useless banning the meeting in terms of the Riotous Assemblies Act — that would only add fuel to the flames. Instead, every available man was to be positioned in a cordon between the Parade and Castle Bridge, and Joubert himself with a picked force would go to the Parade and harangue the meeting if it showed signs of getting out of hand.

"If we could only find that skolly," said Johnson for the ump-teenth time, "we would have nothing to worry about. What is Rolf doing, Dirk?"

Joubert shrugged. "I don't know. I telephoned his boarding house a little while back, but he'd gone out. I hope the old man manages to pull something out of the bag."

As though in answer, the telephone rang, and Rolf le Roux was at the other end of the line.

"I have just seen this leaflet," he said, "and I do not like it. I hope no bloodshed comes of this meeting."

"Forget about that," said Joubert. "The important thing is, can you find the skolly?"

"He will not worry you any more after 7.30 tonight."

"But can't you get hold of him earlier, uncle? You realise if we produce him before the morning there will be no trouble on the Parade. Will it help if I come down?"

"No, Dirk, it is not as easy as that. If you look for the skolly you will never find him. He must be smoked out into the open, and the earliest that can be done is 7.30. But I will tell you what — send Johnson with a couple of plain–clothes men and a car to the Pinkney Hotel in Long Street at seven o'clock. Let them park round the corner in Hout Street until I call them. Then if it is necessary we can rush straight down to the Parade."

And with that Joubert had to remain content.

❂

The organisation of the meeting followed the same thorough pattern as the distribution of the handbills. At five o'clock a squad of workmen disgorged from a lorry, erected a platform and set up a public–address system. At 5.20 a band stepped on to the dais and began to play — popular songs, marches, even well–known hymns, anything to collect a crowd and keep it there. In the meantime, cars and lorries circulated round the town and suburbs, calling the people to the meeting through amplifiers and megaphones. At six o'clock the crowd was already jamming the Parade, and at the microphone a man with a beautiful tenor voice was leading community singing.

Between songs a woman stepped forward to the microphone. "Be patient, friends," she called to them. "This is not a matter to be treated lightly or to be rushed over. We are waiting for the chief speaker of the evening, and when you hear who he is, you will realise he is worth waiting for. The man I am talking about is Machiel Beukes."

There was a prolonged burst of cheering from the crowd, and Joubert felt his heart sink. Beukes was a brilliant orator, a shrewd politician, but his one emotional blind–spot — his colour prejudice — made him, from the police point of view, the worst possible man to address such a meeting.

The music went on, and the singing and the announcements, then a chairman was elected. Joubert saw Beukes' car arriving, and rushed to be the first to speak to the politician. He introduced himself. "Mr. Beukes, we are here in force and our orders are to fight any form of violence with every means at our command. I hope you will see that we have no trouble tonight."

Beukes looked at him through narrowed eyes and smiled at him urbanely. "I think we can promise you, Inspector," he said, "that if there is violence tonight, the people here will not be the ones to strike the first blow."

There was something in the way the words were spoken that made Joubert, if possible, even more worried.

A group of young men came from the crowd, lifted Beukes to their shoulders, and bore him exultantly through the cheering mob. As he reached the platform, the band struck up the South African national anthem, and the tenor led the people into song.

In the hush after the last bar, Beukes stepped to the microphone and began to speak. His voice was easy, compelling: he started off with a few homely jokes and sentiments and in a matter of moments every individual in the crowd felt at one with the man on the platform. Then he launched into an attack on the government, nonetheless virulent for being softly–spoken and interlarded with quiet humour.

He started to deal with colour and race problems and his tone changed. Again he did not use violent diatribe. He spoke about his sons and his unmarried daughter, and what plans he had for them, and again the crowd hung on his words — they were its sons and its daughter — then: "But if the government carries on with its present policy," he said, "then one day my sons will be cleaning the shoes of a Coloured master, my daughter will be the housemaid of a black man!"

With consummate artistry he paused to drink a glass of water, and the tension leapt through the throats of the mob in a roar of anger. Someone — a woman — screamed hysterically: "Are you men? Where are your rifles?" And somewhere in the mass of humanity a great chant arose: "Burn down District Six, burn down District Six!"

Joubert, rallying his men about him preparatory to taking action, saw Beukes gain silence with a single gesture.

"No," he said. "No violence. It is true that the skollies have declared war on us, but the government no doubt looks very liberally on this declaration. They have even sent the police here to see that we behave ourselves.

"I know what the clever men in the Cabinet are thinking. They are thinking that perhaps the skollies do not mean what they say, and that nothing further will happen if we just leave them alone. But do you know what I say? I say that even if the government is right, then matters should not be left as they are — the argument should be settled by a test.

"And, friends, we can provide that test. I say that all of us here should leave now and march through the streets of District Six — not to make trouble, understand me, but to see whether the skollies meant it when they said they would kill on sight every white man they came across. We, friends, will go in peace, and we will be very fair. We will forget all about what has happened in the past, and if the skollies are respectful and let us pass, then I will go home happy that the government was right and my fears were unfounded. But if the skollies attack one of our number, if even by their attitude they show that they would like to attack, then we must give them a lesson, once and for all, who is the master in this land."

He paused, and then added: "I now have a formal motion to that effect."

At that moment Joubert was hoisted by his men on to the platform. "I insist on speaking," he told the chairman, and saw Beukes listening.

Beukes said: "This is a democratic meeting," and went again to the microphone. "Friends," he said, "the officer in charge of the police is here, and would like to speak to you. I want you to give him a good hearing. The man is here to keep the peace. He is doing his duty. He wishes to speak against the motion — I have no objection. All I would like you remember is this — it is not violence we are advocating but self–defence — and then only if it is necessary."

Joubert came forward as he stepped back. "You have been told one side of the question," he said. "I will tell you the other. Do you know why your feelings are high now? Because you are angered against the skolly who stole the diamonds. Surely you can't visit on a whole people the sins of one man?"

His clipped accents fell flat after the smoothness of Beukes' oratory. Someone yelled: "What about the declaration of war?"

Joubert said: "This declaration of war, as you call it, came from the skollies because they thought they were being unjustifiably attacked. It was wrong, of course, but their feelings were high, as yours are high now. If you set out, as has been proposed, to march through District Six, it will be a direct provocation, and violence will be inevitable. Put yourselves in their place. Imagine what you would do now if the skollies came marching down Darling Street. I warn you, if you persist in this idea, blood will flow. Rather than let you pass, my men, who are between here and District Six, have orders to shoot."

A voice yelled: "Now the government wants to help the skollies against the people!" but over all it was as though a great curtain of unease had fallen.

Beukes, his face vivid, elbowed Joubert from the microphone. "Do not believe a word he has said," he told the crowd. "Whatever orders may have been given, remember the men in uniform are our blood brothers. I warn their commandant, and I warn him now before you all, that we are going into District Six, and we are going in peace. We will raise our hand only against an attacker, whether he is a skolly or a policeman. And, Mr. Commandant, remember this — if you give the order to fire on a peaceful procession, you will be committing cold–blooded murder. You — you who are so quick to jump to the defence of the skollies the moment you believe they are threatened — what have you done for our defence and that of our women and children? This skolly whom you say is to blame for our anger — what have you done about him? Your men should not be here, with peace–loving people, but in District Six, among the skollies, looking for the criminal who has done so much harm!"

At the psychological moment of the roar of approval from the crowd, Joubert saw Johnson waving urgently to him from the window of a car that had been driven as close as possible to the platform.

It was his turn now. With steely grip he wrenched the microphone to him and said very loudly and clearly: "The police have done their duty. The skolly is under arrest." Then, as the crowd assimilated what he had said and quietened, he went on. "Now you can feel how the position has altered, I ask Mr. Beukes this: let him come with me, and I will prove that the skolly is under lock and key. Then I think that he will agree, that after this, to march on District Six would be an injustice, and any blood that would be shed by such a march would be his responsibility."

A voice called out: "Don't go, Machiel! He wants to arrest you," and Beukes hesitated.

"If the police have this skolly," he said over the microphone, "and they have proof of it, then why should I go with them? Let them bring that proof here!"

❂

Rolf le Roux came clambering up the side of the dais. "I am bringing the proof," he said very calmly to Beukes and took the microphone as though it was his natural right. And there was a force of personality about the man that let him do it uninterrupted and even, in that one gesture, convince the crowd that he was honest and sincere.

"Friends," he said, "I am an old lawyer and used to making speeches, and now for the first time in my life I find it hard to start. You see, I am supposed to come and give you proof that the skolly who committed all these crimes is safe in gaol, but I can't do that for a very particular reason. There never was such a skolly. But I can tell you this — the people who are responsible for those crimes, they are in the cells — oh yes — and it will be a good many years before they get out."

The crowd was quiet; only one voice shouted: "Don't speak in riddles!"

"Riddles!" said Rolf. "If you thought with your brains instead of your blood there would be no riddles for you.

"Look, friends, not only to give you information but also to calm yourselves, let us go over these crimes step by step. The first that was made public was the theft of the diamonds, then we were told that the same skolly had been responsible for two previous crimes. We knew it was the same skolly because the descriptions were all the same — the methods, the height, the complexion and the mole shaped like a map of South America on his face.

"Think about this mole for a moment, friends. When I thought about it, and the rest of the description, I said it reminded me of the face of the sphinx — not because it was so inscrutable or mysterious, but because it was so unchanging. Every person who has seen the skolly gave precisely the same description.

"I have told you I am an old lawyer, and one thing I have learned in the Courts is that two independent witnesses will never describe the same thing in exactly the same terms. Yet there are four people who do not know each other, who saw the same thing at different times and at different places and yet all describe a peculiarly–shaped mole as being like a map of South America. Why didn't one of them think it was like a tear–drop or a comma or a map of Africa or India? There can be only one explanation — that all four people concerned did know each other and had agreed on a single description."

❂

The atmosphere of the meeting suddenly changed from

emotionalism to almost that of a study class. Even the hecklers became orthodox questioners. A woman asked: "Why should this have been done?"

"Why, indeed," said Rolf. "There can be only one reason — that no such skolly really existed. Obviously, these people who complained of the crime did it for a purpose — to create the character of the skolly in advance, so Breel's story of the theft of the diamonds would be believed. And if they did so conspire, then it is because they themselves are the real thieves of the diamonds."

In an effort to tighten his hold on the meeting Beukes stepped forward. "There is no proof here," he said, "there is only speculation. You are bringing grave allegations against four people, but not one scrap of genuine evidence to support your theory. Must we believe that these people conspired together just because you say so? Proof — that is what we want — and if you cannot give it to us, then we will know that you are lying to gain time — a police trick to protect the skollies!"

The crowd showed signs of restiveness again, there were one or two shouted slogans, but before Rolf's obvious self–possession the noises died.

"My friend is still thinking with his blood," said Rolf. "It is not so long ago since I practised law that I have forgotten that proof is needed. And I have it, listen — and I will tell you what it is.

"I have here three notes, all typewritten. The first one is addressed to Breel, and reads: 'Must see you urgently — unexpected crisis. Bring Miss C with you. Come to Pinkney Hotel at 7.15 to–night and hand this note as proof of your identity to stout man without jacket waiting just outside main entrance. He will show you to room where you must wait for me. Be sure you are not followed.' It is signed 'J. Bingham.' Now, the other two notes are almost the same wording, and signed 'J. M. Breel.' I will not read them to you, but I will hand them to Mr. Beukes on your behalf."

Beukes scrutinised them, and then stepped forward with a triumphant smile. "One little thing only still troubles me," he said, and his voice was loaded with sarcasm. "Why should all the notes have the same wording? If these allegations are true, is it reasonable for Breel to send a note back to Bingham with the same wording as the one he received? The signatures are all different, true, but there is only one explanation that fits all the facts. It is a trick," he roared suddenly, "a clumsy trick to make fools of you — and the signatures on these notes have been forged!"

Even before the crowd could react, Rolf was back at the microphone. "Of course they were forged," he said, and the amplifiers brought out the full contempt in his tones. "I did it myself. I typed the notes on my own typewriter, and then I traced the signatures from the statements made by these people to the police. But that is not the important point. What matters is that after receiving these notes, all four people came as directed to the Pinkney Hotel. They were arrested there by Detective–Sergeant Johnson, who is now down there in that car. With him is also the messenger who delivered all three notes. There is your proof — proof positive that these people knew each other and had conspired together. The rest follows from that fact."

He glanced around him for a moment. "I see even Mr. Beukes appears to be satisfied. And now," he added in firmer tones, "I think we have had enough of this nonsense. You see how, because four criminals had a clever idea, the lives of hundreds have been endangered. You are learning what I have known for a long time — that violence begets violence. It is not only those who live by the sword that die by the sword — innocents perish with them. You have had enough today of blood heat and emotion. And I hope that now you will not be marching off to provoke more quarrels but, like me, will go home to your families and your beds."

He stepped off the platform. There was no applause but despite the fact that Beukes had begun a further impassioned speech, the mass of the crowd began to break off in little groups, in twos and threes, moving towards the bus stops, where they gathered again, but this time in orderly queues.

And Joubert noticed that far above the amplifiers still roaring at the handful of people who remained, there were two clouds, a large one and a small one, and they reminded him of the skolly and his dog. Even as he looked the south–easter whirled over the mountain, caught the clouds, puffed them into myriad wisps and drove them, scattered and lost, behind the stars.

❀

FOOTNOTE:

In 1948, during a general election in South Africa, the racialist Nationalist Party, under Dr D.F. Malan, defeated the United Party of Field–Marshal Jan Smuts, and gained control of the government of South Africa. This provided an enormous shock to those white South Africans — a not inconsiderable minority of about 45 per cent — who were basically humanitarian in their outlook.

There was some panic planning to oppose the new regime. I was contacted by a friend in Johannesburg who was engaged in floating a new magazine pledged to underline the basic evils of Apartheid. He asked me if I could provide him with a short story appropriate to the aims of his proposed publication. At that time I was an accredited Lobby Correspondent for a national newspaper, so I knew my politics pretty well. The story above was my answer to the assignment.

As things turned out, the new magazine never saw the light of day, but I managed to get it printed in another national magazine. I know the tale succeeded, because from then on whatever I did or said was carefully monitored by the Special Branch (forerunners of the infamous B.O.S.S.) and I was harassed by then in one way or another until I left that unhappy country in November 1962.

There is another unique feature about the tale. All the facts are authentic in the sense that the information about the Skollies is completely true. There is a Globe Gang, and in truth its leaders were named Whitey and Telegraph. There was a rival gang called the Jesters, and each had its own territory. To the police and the newspapers they were violent criminals, but to most of the Coloured community they were a benevolent organisation in much the same way as the Cosa Nostra in Italy. For a while, there was even a gang called the Goofies, who operated with large trained dogs, like the skolly in the story. There were 16 of them, and for a while they created a reign of terror among the Coloured. Then the Globe and the Jesters had an emergency meeting. Two mornings later, the corpses of 16 large dogs were found in various portions of the notorious District Six in Cape Town. Their owners simply disappeared.

I modeled the character of Machiel Beukes on J.D. Strydom, who succeeded Malan as leader of the Nationalist Party and as Prime Minister. The things he said at the meeting in the story are identical with what he said regularly at political rallies I reported prior to the 1948 election.

– Peter Godfrey

LITTLE FAT MAN

Have you ever seen the drawing of a face which, when turned around, becomes an entirely different drawing of another quite different face? Well, something like that happens to this story.

Normally, the case would never have been deemed important enough to bring to Lieutenant Joubert's attention, but the young man with the American accent was so flustered and so determined to have his problem dealt with by nobody but 'the Chief' that eventually Sergeant Coetzee, having failed to draw any information out of him, took him up to the room in Caledon Square where Joubert was enjoying a cup of tea with Rolf le Roux and Detective–Sergeant Johnson.

The young man declined the offer of a cup, but gracefully sprawled himself in the proffered easy chair. He introduced himself as Jefferson Carlisle. He was obviously anxious to come to the crux of his business, and his how–do's to the others were completely perfunctory.

Joubert, half amused and half irritated at his manner, said: "Well, Mr. Carlisle?"

"Listen, Chief, I'm being haunted," said the young man.

Joubert had visions of the psychopathic ward. "Really?" he said, "and what does the ghost look like?"

The other grinned. "Pretty substantial," he said. "He's a little fat man with heavy horn–rimmed glasses, and he's been haunting me for over three months. And he's not dead — far from it."

Joubert said: "Oh."

"It wasn't so bad while I was on the move," said Carlisle, "but I don't fancy it now that I've got to spend over a month in this burg. Normally, if it hadn't been for those letters, I'd think he was a con–man following me and waiting for a break — "

"Just a minute," interrupted Joubert, "what letters are you talking about? Look, what about telling us the story from the

117

beginning?"

"Sure," said Carlisle. "Sorry, I guess I was running away with myself. Well, this is how it happened.

"I've got a downtown house in New York, in a spot where it's fairly quiet — at least as quiet as anywhere in New York can be. On account of the fact that my Pop cleaned up on some Texas oil wells, I don't have to work unless I want to. On the morning I'm talking about, I was sitting upstairs typing a letter on my portable, when a stone was thrown through the window.

"The rock crashing on the floor next to my desk startled me, and as a result I felt riled. When I looked down to see what it was, though, I saw a piece of paper tied round it. Here it is."

He handed to Joubert a sheet of cheap notepaper, which he had fished out of his wallet. By means of complete words and individual letters cut from newspapers, a message had been pasted on it. There was no signature or sender's address, and the date was conveyed by the dateline of the *New York Times* of August 21.

The message read, "Forget what you saw in the lane yesterday. Memory will be fatal. I will be watching."

Joubert passed it around to the others.

"What is this reference to the thing you saw in the lane?" asked Rolf.

"Search me! It had no sense for me then, and it's got no sense for me now. The wording of the note, the whole incident, was so like something out of a pulp magazine that my suspicions then didn't travel further than some kid or other."

Johnson asked, "You mean your suspicions widened later?" but Joubert interrupted.

"Go on with your story," he said.

"Sure. Well, I guess I let a good few seconds slip by before I went to the window and leaned out. There were only four people in sight. Almost below me there was a blonde talking to a fair–haired guy, a few yards beyond them a cop was moving slowly on his beat, and some distance further there was a little fat guy with horn–rims and a walking stick.

"I don't know why I took such particular notice of the fat guy, except maybe he was the only one of the four who didn't seem to be doing anything. He was standing and staring at something across the street, but when I followed his gaze, I couldn't see anything worth looking at.   Whatever the reason, I took him in pretty thoroughly, and I had quite a clear picture of him in my mind even after I'd turned back into the room.

"Maybe some sixth sense warned me there was more in the set–up than just a kid's joke; maybe the start I'd got had set my nerves working — I don't know. But all of a sudden I got an urge to get out of the States and do a spot of traveling for a couple of months. At any rate, I believe in playing my hunches so I went down town and booked a seat on a jet leaving next morning.

"I've developed the habit of sleeping on long plane trips, and this time was no exception. I hardly noticed the other passengers on the take–off and during the journey, but when we disembarked at London airport I saw someone amongst the other passengers who looked somehow familiar. When I was going through the Customs, I noticed him again, getting into a taxi, and suddenly I realised who it was. It was the little fat man."

Carlisle paused long enough to hand out cigarettes and pass his lighter to Rolf for his pipe.

"I still didn't see the significance," he went on, "until the next morning, when I found this note had been pushed under the door of my hotel room." He handed over another slip of cheap paper on which had been pasted the dateline of an English journal, and the cryptic message, 'Silence pays, speech slays.' This time there was no comment from the others.

Carlisle went on to describe how he had immediately changed hotels, keeping a vigilant eye open for the little fat man, but he had not seen him.

"I booked in at the Carlford, just off Bloomsbury Square," he said, "and after I had been there a week without seeing the guy, I began to think I'd shaken him off. Then this letter came to me through the post."

The third missive followed the by now familiar pattern. It bore the dateline of the *Daily Telegraph* and the wording was, "Remember to forget."

✪

"That shook me some," said Carlisle. "I began to think that maybe I had been wrong in connecting the letters with the little fat guy, and then I saw him at breakfast. At least, I'd just sat down, and he was just leaving, but he passed within ten yards of me and I was pretty damned certain. I asked the waiter who he was, and he told me he didn't know his name but his room number was 304. After breakfast I went and looked him up in the register. He was listed as Rufus K. Heiderberg, of New York, and he'd checked out ten minutes previously. Right then I decided my own travels would have to start again."

Joubert asked, "Why didn't you take the letters to the police?"

"Search me," said Carlisle, and then added, "Of course I should have. It was just that I looked on the letters not as something criminal but as a nuisance. It looked like the work of a nut to me. And then, of course, there was an element of competition about it. I was wondering how far this guy would follow me, and whether it wouldn't be possible for me to shake him off. At any rate, I decided to go, and I went... "

He went next to Paris, he told them. After he had been there three days a taxi passed him in the street, and the little fat man was peering at him through the window. He hired a car the next day and drove round and round until he was sure he was not being followed, and then struck out for a little junction where he caught a slow train to the south. Two nights after he arrived at Marseilles, another of the pasted notes was waiting for him at his hotel. There was no message this time, just the dateline of a local newspaper, but that was quite enough. Four hours later he was an unexpected passenger on a little Greek tramp bound for Suez.

At the American Express in Cairo he found a letter addressed to him. He slit it open and withdrew another of the pasted notes, bearing the dateline of the previous day's newspaper. He managed to obtain lists of shipping and airways passengers who had arrived during the last three days. It did not take him long to find the name of Rufus K. Heiderberg.

"It was getting me down," said Carlisle. "The way the guy kept on my heels was unnatural, I guess. I should have found out where he was staying and faced up to him, but when I thought it over, I reckoned that if he denied writing the notes and played innocent, I wouldn't be any further, so I cooked up a scheme to shake him off.

"I took the plane to Zurich, then to Frankfurt, down to Rome and then back to Tripoli where I changed to a Dutch line going south, I got off at Kano, stayed two nights, and then went hopping across Africa by Central African Airways to Nairobi. After another week's rest I caught a British jet to Johannesburg,

"To my way of thinking, that finished the matter. In almost two weeks there were no pasted letters, no little fat man. I took a taxi at Jan Smuts Airport and drove straight to the Hotel Crayle. The desk clerk there handed me the register to sign, and as I was taking my pen out of my pocket, my eye idly wandered over the other signatures. The third one from the bottom was Rufus K. Heiderberg, of New York.

"I didn't say a word. I walked out of the hotel and lost myself in the streets as quickly as I could. I spent the night with some hobos on a bench at Park Station, and the next day jumped a Durban–bound train without a reservation. When the guard came round I paid him, but I gave a false name. At Durham, under a different name, I got passage on a coaster to Port Elizabeth, traveled by air to Cape Town under a third name, and booked at the Hilldene Hotel under the name of Jackson.

"That was three days ago and I guessed the little fat man would be Superman in disguise if he caught up with me this time. Then, this morning, I found this letter on the rack."

He handed to Joubert an envelope which had the typewritten address: Mr. J. Jackson, Hilldene Hotel, Cape Town. Inside there was a sheet of cheap paper with pasted message reading, "Lethe waters are safest."

The dateline was that of the *Cape Mail* of the previous day.

"And Heiderberg?" asked Joubert. "Have you seen him?"

Carlisle grinned. "I haven't seen him yet, but I know where he is. He is staying at the same hotel as I am. One of the waiters I questioned told me this and described him and I've checked the signature on the register.

Rolf asked, "After not going to the police all this time, Mr. Carlisle, what made you change your mind now?"

Carlisle shrugged. "Up to now it was a game, but all games come to an end. I don't mind telling you this last letter shook me some. The way the little guy keeps tailing me — it's uncanny. If I knew what he was after, it'd still be OK — I can look after myself — but I don't know, and it's getting me down. It's no good my asking him either — if he answered me in the same language that he uses in his letters I still wouldn't be any wiser. No, it seems to me it's definitely up to the cops to do the rest."

"We'll see what we can do," said Joubert, and telephoned the Hilldene Hotel. After a short conversation with the manager, he passed over a key wallet to Johnson. "Take Mr. Carlisle back," he said. "Use my car. According to the manager Heiderberg is in the lounge. Bring him back with you." He added, "I'm keeping these letters in the meantime, Mr. Carlisle."

"That's OK by me," said Carlisle and touched his forehead in a salute as he followed Johnson out of the room.

❂

Within twenty minutes Johnson was back, and with him was the little fat man.

Heiderberg was a strange contradiction. His clothes, well–cut and of good cloth, and the way he wore them were typical of the unconventional American business man who buys the best, but buys it for comfort, not for show. He wore no waistcoat, for instance, and the trousers of his suit were fastened with a gaily coloured belt. But his voice, his little fat face and watery eyes peering through the spectacles, were those of a Prussian gentleman of the old school.

So were his actions and mannerisms, and they seemed somehow exaggerated by comparison with the informality of his dress.

Joubert thought this when their visitor acknowledged the introductions with a little bow, and the impression was strengthened by the way Heiderberg sat down. Carefully and precisely he sited the exact position of the chair, hitching up his trousers to preserve the crease before allowing his muscles to relax. But the dignified gestures were overdone; the trousers were hitched up much too far for the short socks, and the two pink circles of flesh showing on his legs were a ludicrous finale to such studied actions.

"Why have you brought me here?" he asked. "My passport — there is nothing wrong there, no?"

"Not exactly," said Joubert, who had spent the previous twenty minutes preparing a list of places and dates from the letters Carlisle had left. "We simply want to ask you a few questions."

He read out the details of his list. "Were you in those places at those times?" he asked.

"Yes, but — "

"Can you tell me why?"

Heiderberg, his pink hands, one on top of the other on his belly, seemed to beam good humouredly, but there was a worried under—tone in his voice. "I am traveling. My firm, Heiderberg Inc. in New York, it doesn't need me there any more. I feel I would like to see the world. I am not married, I have money, and I feel I want to travel. Is there anything wrong in that?"

"Not in that. Look, Mr. Heiderberg, I'm going to come to the point. We have received complaints that you have been following a certain person. Can you tell us why?"

"Following? I am not following anybody. No — " He opened his thick lips in a coy smile — "not even the young ladies any more."

"There is no room for doubt," said Joubert abruptly. "If you were in those places and at those times, then you must have been following the person who has complained."

Heiderberg drew himself up. "This person you talk about – has he given reasons why I should follow him?" He waited for a reply, and then, "No? Well, I do not follow anybody. Why should I, Rufus Heiderberg, follow anybody? Yes, once upon a time, a customer for an order — but not today."

Joubert looked down to swallow his impatience and then suddenly thrust one of the pasted—up letters in Heiderberg's face. "Why did you send these?" he asked.

The little fat man peered myopically through his glasses. "I did not send that," he said, and then added suddenly with a new firmness in his tone: "This is a mystery, no? Well, I do not like mysteries — especially on my holiday. And now, gentlemen," he rose to his feet, "you wish to make charges?"

He waited a moment but Joubert did not answer. "Then I will say good afternoon," he said, and bowed very stiffly and slightly, before going out the door.

Joubert turned to Rolf. "Well, old—timer, what do you think?"

The full lips behind the black beard pursed to puff meditatively at the battered pipe. "I do not like it. Coincidence cannot explain this list of yours. And one man does not follow another all these thousands of miles without a purpose. I do not like it," he repeated.

Johnson said, melodramatically, "The old vulture smells blood."

Rolf nodded. "Blood? Perhaps. After all, murder is threatened in those letters."

Joubert said, without decision, "I don't like it either. I'm sending a cable to New York. They may have information about Heiderberg or Carlisle which will shed new light on this matter."

"At the same time," said Rolf, sorting one out from the pile of original letters which Carlisle had received, "ask them if they know of anything that happened in a lane in New York on August 20 which might account for one man threatening to kill another."

"I'll do that," said Joubert, And pulled a pad towards him.

The reply came towards midday the following day.

It read, "Heiderberg head of Heiderberg Inc., drapers, this city. Small man, German–American, fat, aged 53, wears glasses. Semi–retired. Informed by firm he is traveling your country. No police record. Carlisle only son late J. M. Carlisle, oil tycoon. Also traveling. Tall, brown hair, aged 27, no permanent occupation. No police record. Very much interested your other query. Unsolved crime in Makin's Lane, this city, 2.30 p.m. August 20. Chorus girl Frances Vezmar, alias Donovan, strangled to death in broad daylight. No witnesses or clues. Can trace no connection between Heiderberg or Carlisle and deceased, but Vezmar promiscuous and might have known either. Please cable further information."

❂

Joubert had hardly finished reading and had just handed the cable to Rolf when the telephone rang. It was Carlisle. "Say, listen," he said. "I've just had another letter."

"Yes? How does it read?"

"Just three words. 'So you talked.' Make any more sense to you than the others?"

"I think so. Now listen, Carlisle. I want you to answer one or two questions. Have you ever heard of Makin's Lane?"

"Sure. It's a dead end just behind the garages where I park my car in New York. I pass it every day."

"Did you pass it on August 20?"

"Sure. Must have."

"Think carefully. About what time?"

"Well, let me see. August 20 — that's the day before I got the first letter. I remember now. I must have passed it around half–past two."

"Right. Now listen. I think I know why Heiderberg has been following you and I don't want you to take any chances. If you come up here early this afternoon I'll give you all the details."

He rang off, and filled in the gaps in the conversation for Rolf's benefit. "It's as plain as a pikestaff," he said. "Carlisle must have walked past the lane while Heiderberg was murdering the girl. He didn't notice anything out of the ordinary, but Heiderberg didn't know that. His guilty conscience accounts for the rest. That letter this morning seems to show he is preparing some form of action. I'll cable New York for permission to hold Heiderberg pending the extradition warrant."

Rolf shook his head. "I don't like it, Dirk. I think we should go to the hotel now. The man may strike any time."

"But surely, in broad daylight — "

"You forget the sun was shining when the woman was killed."

"That's true. Perhaps you're right. Even though I can't arrest Heiderberg now, I can at least put Carlisle out of danger. Let's go."

They went.

❂

It was apparent even as their car turned into the driveway of the hotel that something was amiss. Someone was shouting at the top of his voice from inside, and a mixed group of waiters and guests were milling in the hotel entrance.

The little effeminate manager said "Thank God," when Joubert introduced himself, and added all in the same breath that a man had been shot in room 77.

They went there, pushing past the morbid sightseers in the passage.

As Carlisle stood up to greet them, there were lines of strain on his face.

The body of Heiderberg lay face–downward on the carpet, and even in death his appearance was paradoxical. The outstretched right hand gripping the ugly–looking knife, conveyed an impression of fierce menace, but the sprawling legs with the strips of pink flesh showing between the bottom of the trouser legs and the tops of the socks were somehow only ridiculous.

"He knocked at the door," Carlisle explained, "and when I called 'come in', he rushed me with the knife. Luckily I'd taken your advice to watch out, and I had my pistol handy. I'm a good shot," he added unnecessarily.

Rolf's voice came then, as though he was reading an epitaph. He said: "Poor little fat man."

Carlisle echoed him. "Poor? What do you mean?"

"I mean I came just too late to save him," said Rolf, "but there is still one thing I can do. His murderer will not go free, I can promise you."

"Murderer?" said Carlisle. "I've told you I killed the man. He came at me with the knife, and I shot him. But that's not murder."

Joubert was also uneasy. "Listen, Oom — "

"No, Dirk, you listen. You remember the time–table you drew up? You were quite right when you thought that if two people were in all those places at the same time, coincidence was out of the question. One must have been following the other. You thought only that Heiderberg had been following Carlisle; I saw that it could quite easily be the other way round. After we had interviewed Heiderberg, I saw the second alternative was by far the most likely."

Joubert asked: "Why?"

"Because Heiderberg was short–sighted. Do you realise how much work with the eyes is necessary to keep on a man's heels so completely? It is not impossible, you must note, but it is most unlikely — much less likely than that Carlisle was the follower."

Carlisle's face was tense and angry, but he made an effort to retain the nonchalance in his voice. "At the risk of waking you from your pipe–dream," he said, "I want to remind you of a couple of things. First there's the question of those letters."

Rolf said, "Yes, the letters. Of course, again it is possible that Heiderberg sent them to you, as it is possible that he was following you. But I do not think the method of cutting out words and letters from a newspaper and pasting them on a sheet of paper is one that would be chosen by a short–sighted man. It is far more likely that you sent them to yourself."

"Likely — unlikely!" Carlisle's voice was full of venom. "What about some proof for a change? Why should I send such letters to myself, and if I did, why should I take them to the police?"

"I will tell you why. On August 20 you cold–bloodedly strangled a girl to death in Makin's Lane. As you were doing it, or more likely as you were coming out of the lane, a little fat man passed and looked in your direction. It was very casual, and he probably didn't even notice you, but you couldn't be sure, could you?

"You followed him, yes, so closely that you could see his every reaction, and you realised after the evening papers came out that he did not associate the casual meeting with the crime. But the cold hand of doubt still gripped you, didn't it? The human mind plays funny tricks. Some day — any day — another little thing might happen — anything — and Heiderberg would remember and understand. While he lived he was the only possible person who could link you with the crime. There was only one way to be absolutely sure — the little fat man must die.

"Your plan probably came to you when you heard he was catching the 'plane overseas — the plan to send yourself fake letters, build up a circumstantial case against the little fat man, so that when you finally did kill him you could bolster up your plea of self–defence. And you came to us because you wanted the police as the chief witnesses for the defence."

"That sure is some story," said Carlisle. "You must have slept overtime to dream it up. But go on — let's have the rest of it. If I did kill the dame and had the brains to think up a slick scheme like that, how come I'd be such a mug as to let you get your hooks on Heiderberg and give him a chance to spill the beans about what he was supposed to have seen in the lane?"

"There was so little chance of that," said Rolf, "that the risk was well worth it. If the newspaper reports of the murder hadn't stimulated Heiderberg's memory, what chance was there of an oblique reference to a lane in the original pasted–up letter doing it? No, your only danger lay in Heiderberg's recognising you personally, and putting two and two together. You must have kept well out of his way while you were following him, and you were determined to kill him before there was the slightest chance of him pointing you out to the police. And even there," he added, "the danger was only in your mind. He was short–sighted, remember. He probably never even saw you that day."

Carlisle said, "One thing more, before I let myself get good and mad. I take it that reference to the lane helped you trace back to the dame's murder. Do you think, if I'd done it, I'd be fool enough to point to the matter so obviously?"

"It was necessary," said Rolf. "You had to show some logical reason why Heiderberg was following you. And that was very clever and very subtle. You reasoned that when the police had their attention drawn to the first murder they would conclude that Heiderberg was threatening you because he was the murderer and he thought that you had some evidence against him. When you gave that little touch over the telephone that you passed the lane at the time the murder was being committed, you thought your plan was going very nicely."

"Aw, nuts! Theories, suppositions — the heck with it! You haven't got a single shred of evidence. You can't have — because it isn't true. What happened today bears me out fully. I've given you the facts — he knocked on the door, rushed me with a knife and I shot him. There he lies — knife and all. Now theorise your way round that one!"

Rolf asked, "Did you touch the body at all?"

"No."

"Then you have convicted yourself, Carlisle. I will tell you what actually happened. You somehow got Heiderberg in the room, and then, because you are not so confident of our aim as you tried to imply just now, you got him to sit on a chair in front of your table before you took careful aim and fired. Then you jumped up quickly, pulled the chair away so he slumped onto the floor. You put the knife in his hand."

The muscles in Carlisle's face were moving. "More theories, Sherlock. Prove it."

Rolf said, "I will." He turned to Joubert, "Do you remember, Dirk, when Heiderberg sat down in your office, how he hitched up his trousers? He pulled them right over the tops of his socks, and that is how they are pulled up now. There are only two ways in which that could have happened — either he sat down, or else the body had been lifted and dragged by the ankles. In either eventuality, the story Carlisle has told is a lie. And if this story of his is a lie... "

He reached forward suddenly and clamped his stubby fingers over the wrist of the hand Carlisle was stretching forward to the pistol on the table. There was no trace of effort on his face, but Carlisle winced with pain from the force that was being applied.

"I am not a violent man," said Rolf, "but I can understand a violent crime, done on the spur of the moment and with passion. I cannot condone a murder such as you have committed. If I let you get that gun, Dirk here will shoot you, and you will die suddenly and quickly. I do not think that would be fair to Heiderberg. You must die, yes, but only after all the coils of evidence against you have been so carefully wound that there is no escape. Just as you did to him. And when the final trap falls, and the strangling noose breaks your neck, yes, perhaps then the little fat man will be avenged."

THE FLUNG-BACK LID

This is a variation on the classic "sealed room" story. Here the sealed room is a cable car. A man is alive in the car when it leaves the summit of Table Mountain. When it reaches half way, people in the ascending car see the man is slumped in death, with a large knife protruding from his back. There is nobody with him in the car. How was he killed? Why? And who did it?

All that day, the last day of March, the cableway to the top of Table Mountain had operated normally. Every half hour the car on the summit descended, and the car below ascended, both operating on the same endless cable. The entire journey took seven minutes.

Passengers going up or coming down gawked at the magnificent panorama over the head of the blase conductor in each car. In his upper–station cabin the driver of the week, Clobber, hunched conscientiously over his controls during each run, and was usually able to relax for the rest of the half hour.

In the restaurant on the summit, Mrs. Orvin worked and chatted and sold curios and postcards and buttered scones, and showed customers how to post their cards in the little box which would ensure their stamps would be canceled with a special Table Mountain franking.

In the box–office at the lower station, the station master, Brander, sold tickets for the journey, and chatted with the conductor who happened to be down at the time, and drank tea.

Then, at 5.30 p.m., the siren moaned its warning that the last trip of the day was about to commence. Into the upper car came the last straggling sightseers, the engineer on duty, Mrs. Orvin, and the conductor, Skager. Alone in the lower car was the other conductor, Heston, who would sleep overnight on the summit.

Then two bells rang, and the cars were on their way. For the space of seven minutes Clobber and the Native labourer, Ben, were the only two on top of the mountain. Then the cars docked, and Heston stepped jauntily on to the landing platform.

He joined Clobber, but neither spoke. Their dislike was mutual

130

and obvious. They ate their evening meal in silence.

Clobber picked up a book. Heston took a short walk, and then went to bed.

Some hours later, he woke up. Somewhere in the blackness of the room he could hear Clobber snoring softly.

Heston bared his teeth. Snore now, he thought, snore now. But tomorrow...

The night began to grow less black. The stars faded first, then the lights far below in the city also winked out. The east changed colour. The sun rose.

It was tomorrow.

❂

Brander came into the room which housed the lower landing platform, and peered myopically up along the giant stretch of steel rope.

The old Cape Coloured, Piet, was sweeping out the car which had remained overnight at the lower station — the right–hand car. He said: "Dag*, Baas Brander."

"Dag, Piet," said Brander.

Two thousand feet above, the upper station looked like a doll's house, perched on the edge of the cliff. The outlines of Table Mountain stood deep–etched by the morning sun. On the flat top of the elevation there was no sign of cloud — the tablecloth, as people in Cape Town call it — and there was no stirring of the air.

Brander thought: Good weather. We will be operating all day.

Piet was sweeping carefully, poking the broom edgeways into the corners of the car. He noticed Brander looking at him, and his old parchment flat–nosed face creased suddenly into a myriad of grins. "Baas Dimple is the engineer today," he said. "The car must be very clean."

"That's right, Piet," said Brander. "Make a good job for Baas Dimble. You still have twenty minutes."

❂

* Afrikaans: "Good day."

In the upper station, Clobber settled himself in his chair in the driver's cabin, and opened the latest issue of *Armchair Scientist*. He had just about enough time, he reckoned, to finish the latest article on the new rocket fuels before the test run at nine–thirty.

Line by line his eyes swallowed words, phrases and sentences. Then, interrupting the even flow of his thoughts, he felt the uneasy consciousness of eyes staring at the back of his neck. He had an annoying mental image of Heston's thin lips contorting in a sardonic smile.

He turned. It was Heston, but this time his face was unusually serious. "Did I interrupt you?" he asked.

"Oh, go to hell," said Clobber. He marked the place in his magazine, and put it down. He asked: "Well?"

"I wanted a few words with you," said Heston.

"If it's chit–chat you're after, find someone else."

Heston looked hurt. "It's... well, it's rather a personal problem. Do you mind?"

"All right. Go ahead."

"I'm a bit worried about the trip down."

"Why? You know as well as I do that nothing can go wrong with the cable."

"No, it's not that. It's just... Look, Clobber, I don't want you to think I'm pulling your leg, because I'm really very serious. I don't think I'm going to get down alive. You see, yesterday was my birthday — I turned thirty–one and it was 31 March — and I had to spend last night up here. Now, I'm not being superstitious or anything, but I've been warned that the day after my birthday I'd not be alive if my first trip was from the top to the bottom of the mountain. If I hadn't forgotten, I'd have changed shifts with someone, but as it is... "

"Look here, Heston, if you're not bluffing, you're the biggest damned fool — "

"I'm not bluffing, Clobber. I mean it. You see, I haven't got a relation in the world. If anything does happen, I'd like to see that each of the men gets something of mine as a sort of keepsake. You can have my watch. Dimble gets my binoculars — "

"Sure, sure. And your million–rand bank account goes to Little Orphan Annie. Don't be a damned fool. Who gave you this idiotic warning, anyway?"

"I had a dream — "

"Get to hell out of here, you little rat! Coming here and — "

"But I mean it, Clobber — "

"Get out! It would be a damned good thing for all of us if you didn't reach the bottom alive!"

❄

Dimble, neat and officious but friendly, arrived at the lower station wagon, and with him were Skager and Mrs. Orvin.

Brander shuffled forward to meet them.

"Nice day," said Dimble. "What's your time, Brander? Nine–twenty–five? Good, our watches agree. Everything ship–shape here? Fine."

Skager scratched a pimple on his neck.

Mrs. Orvin said: "How's your hand, Mr. Brander?"

The station–master peered below his glasses at his left hand, which was neatly bound with fresh white bandages. "Getting better slowly, thanks. It's still a little painful. I can't use it much, yet."

"Don't like that Heston," said Dimble. "Nasty trick he played on you, Brander."

"Perhaps it wasn't a trick, Mr. Dimble. Perhaps he didn't know the other end of the iron was hot."

"Nonsense," said Mrs. Orvin. "He probably heated it up, specially. I can believe anything of him. Impertinent, that's what he is."

"Even if he did do it," said Brander, "I can't bear any hard feelings."

Dimble said: "You're a religious man, eh, Brander? All right in its way, but too impractical. No good turning the other cheek to a chap like Heston. Probably give you another clout for good measure. No, I'm different. If he'd done it to me, I'd have my knife into him."

"He'll get a knife into him one of these days," said Skager, darkly. He hesitated. "He'll be coming down in the first car, won't he?"

"Yes," said Brander.

"And it's just about time," said Dimble. "We'd better get in our car. After you, Mrs. Orvin. So long, Brander."

"Goodbye, Mr. Dimble — Mrs. Orvin — Skager."

❂

Heston came through the door leading to the landing platform at the upper station. In the car, the Native Ben was still sweeping.

"Hurry up, you lazy black swine," said Heston. "What in hell have you been doing with yourself this morning? It's almost time to go, and you're still messing about. Get out of my way."

The Native looked at him with a snarl. "You mustn't talk to me like that. I'm not your dog. I've been twenty years with this company, and in all that time nobody's ever spoken to me like that — "

"Then it's time someone started. Go on — get out!"

Ben muttered: "I'd like to — "

"You'd like to what? Come up behind me when I'm not looking, I suppose? Well, you won't get much chance for that. And don't hang around — voetsak!"*

From the driver's cabin they heard the two sharp bells that indicated that the cars were ready to move. Ben stepped aside. As the upper car began to slide down and away Heston went through the door, up the short flight of stairs and into the driver's cabin. He looked over Clobber's shoulder at the plate–glass window.

The upper car was then 20 or 30 yards from the station. Both men saw Heston lean over the side of the car, and salute them with an exaggerated sweep of his right arm. Both men muttered under their breath.

As the seconds ticked by, the two cars approached each other in mid–air.

In the ascending car Dimble looked at the one that was descending with a critical eye. Suddenly, he became annoyed. "That fool," he said. "Look how he's leaning out over the door. Dangerous... "

His voice tailed off. As the cars passed each other, he saw something protruding from Heston's back — something that gleamed silver for an inch or two, and was surmounted by a handle of bright scarlet. Dimble said: "God!" He reached and jerked the emergency brake. Both cars stopped suddenly, swaying drunkenly over the abyss.

*Afrikaans: "Scram!"

Skager moaned: "He's not leaning... "

Mrs. Orvin gulped audibly. "That's my knife," she said, "the one he said... "

○

The telephone bell in the car rang shrilly. Dimble answered it.

"What's the trouble?" came Clobber's voice.

"It's Heston. He's slumped over the door of the car. There seems to be a knife in his back."

"A knife? Hell! He was alive when he left here. He waved to me... What should we do?"

"Hang on a second. Brander, are you on the other end? Have you heard this conversation?"

"Yes, Mr Dimble."

"Okay, Clobber. I'm releasing the brake now. Speed it up a little."

"Sure."

The cars moved again.

At the top, Dimble led the rush up the stairs to the driver's cabin, where Clobber's white face greeted them. They waited.

The telephone rang.

Clobber stretched out a tentative hand, but Dimble was ahead of him.

"I've seen him," said Brander, queerly. "He's dead."

"Are you sure?"

"Yes. He's dead."

"Now look, Brander, we must make sure nothing is touched. Get on the outside phone to the police right away. And let Piet stand guard over the body until they get here, OK?"

"It might be difficult, Mr. Dimble. There are people here already for tickets, so I can't leave here, and Piet is scared. He's said so. I've locked the door leading to the landing stage — won't that be enough?"

"No. If anyone there is curious, they can climb round the side of the station to the car, and possibly spoil evidence. Let me speak to Piet."

"Here he is, Mr. Dimble."

"Hullo, Piet. Now listen — I want you to stand guard on the

landing stage and see nobody touches the car until the police arrive."

"No, Baas. Not me, Baas. Not with a dead body, Baas."

"Oh, dammit. OK, Let me speak to Mr. Brander. Brander? Listen — this is the best plan. Don't sell any tickets — we won't be operating today, anyway. We'll start the cars and stop them halfway so nobody will be able to get near them. In the meantime you telephone the police. Do you get that?"

"Yes, I will telephone the police."

"And give me a ring the moment they are here."

"Yes, Mr. Dimble."

✪

The police came. Caledon Square had sent its top murder team. Lieutenant Dirk Joubert was in charge of the party, and with him was his uncle, Rolf le Roux, the "expert on people" as he jocularly styled himself, the inevitable kromsteel* protruding through the forest of his beard. Happy Detective–Sergeant Johnson was there, Lugubrious Sergeant Botha, Doc McGregor and several uniformed men. They mounted the steps to the lower station building and found Brander waiting for them.

"Where is the body?" asked Joubert.

Brander pointed out the two tiny cars on their thin threads a thousand feet above. "Will you please speak on the internal phone to Mr. Dimble, the engineer in charge, who's at the upper station?" he asked.

"Get him for me," said Joubert.

Brander made the connection, and then handed over the phone.

"Mr. Dimble? I am Inspector Joubert of the Cape Town C.I.D. I want the cable car with the body to be allowed to come down here. What? No, it'd be better if you people stayed on top of the mountain while we do our preliminary work here. I'll ring you when we're ready. Hullo! Just one moment, just bring me up to date on the discovery of the crime — briefly, please. I see. You were going up in the right–hand car, and when you passed the other one at half–way, you saw a knife sticking out of the conductor's back. His name?

---

* Curved Boer pipe.

Heston... yes, I have that. And then? I see. Yes. Yes. And why did you move the car with the body half–way back up the mountain? Mm. No, that's all right — it was a good idea. Right, better get the body back here now."

Almost as soon as he put the receiver down, the cable began to whine.

❂

From the landing–stage they watched the approaching car. Even at some distance they could see the slumped figure quite clearly, with the scarlet splash of the knife handle protruding from its back.

"I can tell you one thing right now," said McGregor. "It's not a suicide."

As the car came closer to the landing–stage, Johnson began checking his photographic and fingerprint equipment.

Brander mumbled: "It is the will of the Lord... "

He looked almost grateful when Joubert said: "There's nothing we can do here, Brander. Let's go into the ticket office. There are one or two questions... "

Rolf went with them.

Joubert said: "I've had the rough details of the story from Mr. Dimble. You were here when the body first came down. Did you examine it?"

"No."

"Why not?"

"He was dead. I could see that."

"And did anyone else come near the body? This Coloured, Piet?"

"No, not Piet. He was afraid. He wouldn't go near the car. He stood at the door until the motors started, though, in case anyone else wanted to go through."

"Anyone else? Who else was here?"

"Well, there was a man and two women — passengers — but they left when I wouldn't sell them tickets."

Joubert tried a new tack. "This Heston, now. Tell me, Brander, what sort of a man was he? Was there anyone working here who hated him?"

Brander hesitated. "I do not like to talk about him. He is dead now. What does it matter what he was like in life?"

Joubert said: "Answer my question. Is there anyone here who hated him?"

"He was not liked," said Brander, "but nobody here hated him enough to kill him."

"No? Someone stuck a knife in his back, all the same. Who could have done it?"

"What does it matter?" said Brander. "He's dead now. Let him rest in peace."

❂

The experts had finished. Two constables carried a long basket clumsily down the steps to a waiting ambulance.

"Well, Doc?" asked Joubert.

"One blow," said McGregor. "A very clean swift blow. No mess. The murderer struck him from behind and above. Either the killer stood on something, or he was a very tall man."

"Or woman?"

"Maybe. I canna say one way or another."

Johnson made his report. "No fingerprints on the knife, Dirk. Couple of blurred smears, that's all. Probably wore gloves."

Joubert said: "All right. Doc, you go back with the body, and do the P.M. If you come up with anything new, telephone me here... Now let's talk to this Coloured, Piet."

But Piet knew nothing. He was old and superstition–ridden. He had not even looked at the body. The nearest he had come to it was to stand on guard on the other side of a closed door.

Joubert phoned Dimble. "We're coming up. What is the signal for starting the car? Two bells — right. I'm not interested in rules about conductors on every trip. We're coming up without one, and the car at the top must come down completely empty. All right — so it's irregular. So is murder. I'll take the responsibility... We'll want to interview you one at a time. Is there a room there we can use? The restaurant? Right. You'll hear the signal in a couple of minutes."

Joubert, Rolf le Roux and Johnson. Four uniformed policemen. Going up in the car in which death had come down.

"I don't think we'll be long," said Joubert. "The solution's on top, obviously."

Rolf said: "How do you make that out?"

"When the cars reached the middle of the run, Heston already had the knife in his back. He was alone in the cable–car. Therefore he must have been killed before he left the summit. One of the men stationed up there is the chap we're looking for."

Rolf looked worried. He said: "I hope you are right."

"Of course I'm right. It's the only possible explanation."

"So you'll start off by concentrating on the men who were on the mountain when the cars started this morning?"

"No, let them stew in their own juice for a while. This Dimble seems a proper fuss–pot — better get him over first."

○

Dimble

"... And so I told Brander to see the body was guarded, and when I found Piet was afraid I told him... "

"Right, Dimble. We've got all that. Now, let me get one thing clear. Apart from Heston, there were two men who stayed overnight at the summit — Clobber, and the Native, Ben?"

"Yes."

"Did either of these two have anything against Heston?"

"Probably. Heston wasn't very likable, you know. But I don't think anyone would murder him."

Joubert said again: "Someone did. Now look, Dimble — to your knowledge did either Clobber or Ben have anything against Heston?"

"Not to my knowledge, no. They may have. For that matter, we all disliked him. He was always doing something... objectionable. Like practical jokes — only there was malice behind them, and he never acted as though he was joking. Never could be sure. Nasty type."

Rolf asked: "Exactly what sort of objectionable actions do you mean Mr Dimble?"

"Well, like putting an emetic in my sandwiches when I wasn't looking. Couldn't prove it was him, though. And burning Brander's hand."

Joubert said: "I noticed his left hand was bandaged. What happened?"

"Heston handed him a length of iron to hold, and his end was all but red–hot."

"I see. So it would appear that both you and Brander had cause to hate the man?"

"Cause, yes, and I must admit I didn't like him. But Brander's different. We were talking about it this morning, and he didn't seem to bear any grudge. He's a religious type, you know."

"So I gathered," said Joubert, drily.

Dimble went on: "And that reminds me — Skager had it in for Heston too. When I mentioned that if it had been my hand he burnt, I'd have my knife in for him, Skager said that one day someone would... Hey! That's ironic, isn't it?"

"Yes," said Joubert. "All right, Dimble. Let's have Skager."

❁

Skager

A pasty, pimply young man, with a chip on his shoulder.

"I didn't mean anything by it, Inspector. It's just an expression. I didn't like him."

"So you didn't like him, and you just used an expression? Doesn't it strike you as strange that a few minutes later Heston did have a knife in his back?"

"I didn't think about it."

"Well, think now, Skager. Why did you hate him?"

"Look, Inspector, I had nothing to do with the murder. How could I have killed him?"

"How do you know how he was killed? I tell you, Skager, I am prepared to arrest any man who attempts to hide his motives... Now answer my question?"

A slight pause of defiance, then —

"Well, I don't suppose it makes any difference. I've got a girlfriend. Some time ago, someone rang her up and warned her not to go out with me because I had an incurable disease. It took me weeks before I could convince her it was a lie."

"And you thought Heston made the phone call?"

"Yes."

"Why?"

"Maybe because he was always making snide remarks about my pimples. Besides, it's just the kind of sneaky trick he would get up to."

"So you hated him, eh, Skager — hated him enough to kill him?"

"Why do you pick on me, Inspector? I know nothing about any murder. Why don't you speak to Mrs. Orvin? At least she recognised the knife... "

❂

Mrs. Orvin

Mrs. Orvin said: "Yes, the knife is mine. My brother–in–law sent it to me from the Congo."

"What did you use it for?"

"Mainly as an ornament. Occasionally for cutting. It was kept on this shelf under the glass of the counter."

"So anyone could have taken it while you were in the kitchen?"

"Yes, that's what must have happened."

"When did you find it was missing?"

"Yesterday afternoon."

"And before that, when did you last notice it?"

"Only a few minutes earlier. I'd been using it to cut some string, and I put it down to attend to something in the kitchen — "

"Was there anyone else in the restaurant at the time?"

"Yes, quite a few people. Four or five tourists and Heston and Clobber."

"Clobber was here?"

"Yes, having his tea. He sat at the far corner table."

"And Heston?"

"At first he was on the balcony, but when I came back from the kitchen he was sitting at this table."

"So when you missed the knife, what did you do?"

"I spoke to Heston... "

Heston looked up innocently at her. "Yes, Mrs. Orvin?"

"Mr. Heston, have you by any chance seen my knife?"

"You mean the big one with the red handle? The voodoo knife? Of course I have. You were using it a minute ago."

"Well, it's gone now. Did you see anyone take it?"

"No, I didn't see anyone take it, Mrs. Orvin, but I know what happened to it all the same."

"What?"

"It suddenly rose in the air, and sort of fluttered out through the door. All by itself... "

"Mr. Heston, you're being stupid and impertinent— "

"But it's true, Mrs. Orvin, it's true. Some of the other people here must have seen it, too. Why don't you ask Clobber?"

Joubert said: "And did you ask Clobber, Mrs. Orvin?"

"Yes."

"And what did he say?"

"He knew nothing about the knife. He was very angry when I told him about Heston."

"Well, thanks, Mrs. Orvin — I think that'll be all for now."

Mrs. Orvin left.

Rolf allowed a puff of smoke to billow through his beard. He said to Johnson: "So now we have a flying voodoo dagger."

"Utter nonsense," said Joubert. "This is murder, not fantasy. Someone wearing gloves killed Heston, and the murder was done on top of the mountain. It can only be one of two — the Native or Clobber. I fancy Clobber."

"You're quite sure, eh?" said Rolf. "What will you say if we find Heston was alive when he left the summit?"

"It just couldn't happen. There is no possible way of stabbing a man alone in a cable–car in mid–journey."

Rolf said: "I still have a feeling about this case... "

"There are too many feelings altogether. What we need are a few facts. Let's send for Clobber."

❂

Clobber

Clobber was pale. He was still wearing the soiled dustcoat he used while driving. Joubert looked at something protruding from the pocket and glanced significantly at Johnson and Rolf.

"Do you always wear cotton gloves?" he asked.

"Yes. They keep my hands clean."

"They also have another very useful purpose. They don't leave fingerprints."

Clobber's face went even whiter. "What are you getting at? I didn't kill Heston. He was alive when he left the summit."

"And dead when he passed the other car half–way down? Come off it, Clobber. He must have been killed up here. Either you or Ben are guilty."

Clobber said, stubbornly: "Neither of us did it. I tell you he was alive when he left."

"That's what you say. The point is, can you prove it?"

"Yes, I think so. After the car had started, when he was about twenty yards out, he leant over the side of the car and waved to me. Ben had just come into my cabin. He saw him too."

"Where was Ben before that?"

"He was with Heston at the car."

"A new gleam came into Joubert's eye. "Look, Clobber," he said, "couldn't Ben have stabbed Heston just as the car pulled away?"

"I suppose he could, but don't forget, Ben was with me when Heston waved."

"Are you sure it was a wave? Couldn't it have been a body wedged upright, and then slumping over the door?"

"No, definitely not. The arm moved up and down two or three times. He was alive. I'm sure of that."

Joubert flung up his hands in a gesture of impatience. "All right, then. Say he was alive. Then how did the knife get in his back half–way down?" Clobber looked harassed. "I don't know. He had an idea... but that's nonsense — "

"Idea? What idea?"

"He told me this morning he didn't expect to get to the bottom of the mountain alive."

Rolf echoed: "Didn't expect?"

"Yes. He said he'd been warned. His thirty–first birthday was yesterday — the 31st of the month — and he'd been told that if he spent last night on top of the mountain, he'd never reach the bottom alive. I thought he was pulling my leg."

"Who was supposed to have told him that?"

"He said it was a dream."

Joubert said: "Oh, my God!" but Rolf's face was serious.

"Tell me, Mr. Clobber," he said, "did Heston ever mention prophetic dreams to you before?"

"Just once. About a month ago."

"And the circumstances?"

"I'd just come off duty, and I was at the lower station with Heston and Brander. Somehow or the other the conversation led to the subject of death... "

Clobber said: "When a man dies, he's dead. Finished. A lot of chemical compounds grouped round a skeleton. No reason to hold a body in awe. The rituals of funerals and cremations are a lot of useless hooey. There should be a law compelling the use of bodies for practical purposes — for transplants, medical research, making fertiliser — anything except burning them up or hiding them in holes in the ground under fancy headstones."

Brander was uneasy. "I don't think I can agree with you... "

"The trouble with you, Brander, is that you're a religious man, which also means you are a superstitious one. Try looking at hard facts. What we do with our dead is not only irrational, it's also economically wasteful.

"Last night I went to a municipal–election meeting. The speaker made what the crowd thought was a joke, but he was really being sensible. He said the wall round Woltemade cemetery was an example of useless spending — the people outside didn't want to get in, and the people inside couldn't get out... What's the matter with you, Brander?"

Heston suddenly interrupted. "You've upset him with all your callous talk. Can't you realise that Brander's a decent religious man who has a proper respect for the dead?"

Brander dabbed his forehead and his lips in an obvious effort to pull himself together. "No... no... it's not just that. This business about the wall and the people inside reminds me of something that's always horrified me. The idea of the dead coming to life. Even the Bible story of Lazarus... you see, ever since I can remember, every now and again I have a terrible nightmare. I'm with a coffin at a funeral, and suddenly from inside the box there's a loud knock... I feel my insides twisting in fear... "

Clobber said, hastily: "Sorry, Brander. Didn't mean to upset you. But if you think about it for a moment, you'll realise the whole thing's a lot of nonsense — the dead coming to life, and things like that. Absolute rubbish."

"Really?" said Heston. "What about Zombies?"

Brander gasped: "What?"

"Zombies. Dead men brought to life by voodoo in the West Indies to work in the fields. And dreams, too. I know all about prophetic dreams."

Clobber was almost spitting with rage. "What do you mean, you know? What are you getting at?"

"I'll tell you some other time," said Heston. "Here's the station wagon, and I'm in a hurry."

Joubert said: "And the next time he mentioned a dream to you was to tell you he wouldn't reach the lower station alive?"

"Yes."

"And now do you believe in prophetic dreams?"

"It's got so I don't know what to believe."

Joubert rose. "Well, I do. There are no prophesies and nothing here except a cleverly planned murder, and God help you if you did it, Clobber — because I'm going to smash your alibi."

"You can't smash the truth," said Clobber. "In any case, why should I be the one under suspicion?"

"One of the reasons," said Joubert, "is that you wear gloves."

Clobber grinned for the first time. "Then you'll have to widen your suspect list. We all wear them up here. Dimble has a pair. Ben, too. And, yes, Mrs. Orvin generally carries kid gloves."

"All right," said Joubert savagely. "That's enough for now. Tell Ben we want to see him."

❂

Ben came, gave his evidence, and went.

"If I could prove that he and Clobber were collaborating," Joubert started, but Rolf stopped him with a shake of his head.

"No, Dirk. There is nothing between them. I could see that. You could see it, too."

"We're stymied," said Johnson. "Apparently nobody could have done it. I examined the cable-car myself, and I'm prepared to swear there's no sign of any sort of apparatus which could explain the stabbing of a man in mid-air. He was alive when he left the top, and dead at the half-way mark. It's just... plain impossible."

"Not quite," said Joubert. "We do know some facts. First, this is a carefully premeditated crime. Secondly, it was done before the car left the summit — "

Rolf said: "No, Dirk. The most important facts in this case lie in what Heston told Clobber — his dream of death — his thirty-first birthday — "

"What are you getting at, Oom?"

"I think I know how and why Heston was killed, Dirk. It's only a theory now, and I do not like to talk until I have proof. But you can help me get that proof... "

❂

The word went round. A reconstruction of the crime. Everyone must do exactly as he did when Heston was killed.

Whispers.

"Who's going to take Heston's place?"

"The elderly chap with a beard: le Roux I think his name is. The one they call Oom Rolf."

"Do you think they'll find out anything? Do you think — ?"

"We'll know soon enough, anyway."

On the lower station Joubert rang the signal for the reconstruction to start. Dimble, Mrs. Orvin and Skager went towards the bottom car. Sergeant Botha went, too.

Rolf le Roux came through the door of the upper landing platform, and looked at Ben sweeping out the empty car.

He said: "Baas Heston spoke to you, and you stopped sweeping?"

"Yes. And then I came out of the car, like this."

"And then?"

"Then we talked."

"Where did Baas Heston stand?"

He got into the car, and stood near the door. Yes, just about there." He paused. "Do you think you will find out who killed him?"

"It is possible."

"I hope not, Baas. This Heston was a bad man."

"All the same, it is not right that he should be killed. The murderer must be punished."

Two sharp bells rang in the driver's cabin. The car began to move. Ben went through the door up the stairs and stood in the cabin with Clobber and Johnson. They saw Rolf lean over and wave with an exaggerated gesture.

Clobber reached to lift a pair of binoculars, but Johnson gripped his arm. "Wait. Did you pick them up at this stage the first time?"

"No. I only used them after the emergency brake was applied,"

"Then leave them alone now."

They watched the two cars crawling slowly across space towards each other.

In the ascending car Dimble peered approvingly at the one which was descending. "That's right," he said to Botha. "He's leaning over the door exactly as Heston... Good God!"

He pulled the emergency brake. Mrs. Orvin sobbed and then screamed.

The telephone rang. Botha clapped the instrument to his ear.

"Everything OK?" asked Johnson.

"No!" said Botha, "no! Something's happened to Rolf. There's a knife sticking out of his back. It looks like the same knife... "

From the lower station Joubert cut in excitedly. "What are you saying, Botha? It's impossible... "

"It's true, Inspector. I can see it quite clearly from here. And he's not moving... "

"Get him down here," said Joubert. "Quick!"

The cars moved again.

In the driver's cabin Johnson, through powerful binoculars, watched the car with the sagging figure go down, down, losing sight of it only as it entered the lower station.

Joubert, with Brander, stood on the landing–stage watching the approaching car. He felt suddenly lost and bewildered and angry.

"Oom Rolf," he muttered.

Brander's eyes were sombre with awe. "The Lord has given," he said, "and the Lord has taken away. Blessed be the name of the Lord."

He and Joubert stepped forward as the car bumped to a stop.

The head of the corpse with the knife in its back suddenly twisted, grinned, said gloatingly: "April fool!"

Brander shivered into shocked action. His arms waved in an ecstacy of panic. His bandaged left hand gripped the hilt of the knife held between Rolf's left arm and his body, and raised it high in a convulsive gesture. Rolf twisted away, but his movement was un-necessary. Joubert had acted, too.

Brander struggled, but only for a second. Then he stood meekly, peering in myopic surprise at the handcuffs clicking round his wrists.

"And that is how Heston was killed," said Rolf. "He died because he remembered today was April the first — All Fools Day — and because he had that type of mind, he thought of a joke, and he played it to the bitter end. A joke on Clobber, on the people in the ascending car, on Brander.

"But to Brander it was not a joke — it was horror incarnate. A dead man come to life. This was infinitely more terrible than the dream he feared of a knock from a coffin. This was like the very lid being suddenly flung open in his face. And his reaction was the typical response to panic when there is no escape — a wild uncon-trollable aggression, striking out in every direction — as he struck out at me when the unthinkable happened again.

"The first time he plunged the knife into Heston. The joke became reality. The dead stopped walking."

"And now you see why there were no fingerprints on the knife. Brander is left–handed — he reached for the hot iron with that hand, remember. So it was burnt and bandaged. Bandages — no fingerprints. The way Heston was crouched, too, explains the angle of the wound."

Joubert said: "So it was not premeditated after all." Then, to Brander: "Why did you not tell the truth?"

Brander said, meekly: "Who would believe the truth?" Then, louder, with undertones of a new hysteria: "The dead are dead. They must rest in peace. Always rest. They are from hell if they walk... "

Then he mumbled, and his voice tailed off as he raised his eyes, and his gaze saw far beyond the mountain and the blue of the sky.

THE PERFUMES OF ARABIA

Shakespearian characters come to life... and death.

ACT 1

Right from the beginning there was an atmosphere about the case where no atmosphere should have existed. The facts were straightforward. The dark–haired man who was about to be murdered came out of the front entrance of the Britannia Palace Hotel, and started to walk up the road. The other man, lurking in the shadows, did not so much follow as stalk him positively. He came up behind his victim, almost at a run, and chopped down with something resembling a truncheon. The attacked man dropped without a sound.

It happened at about 10 p.m. The street was almost deserted — the one eye–witness was in his car 20 yards away. Even so, lights blazing through the glass frontage of Tony's Bar Grill had highlighted the whole affair; a more than adequate description of the murderer had been obtained. Very satisfactory. And yet...

"It was strange, I tell you," said Bruyns, the Cape Coloured taxi driver who had witnessed the incident. "There was something about the red–headed man that was, well funny. The way he moved, like he was bouncing. Like a kid showing off. Sort of made me look at him, even before I knew what he was up to and then, afterwards... You see, he hit the man, and started to move off. Then he stopped suddenly and turned back, and hit the body again. Many times — like in a frenzy. He must have seen me opening the door of my cab, and I'm sure he heard me yell, but he still waited to shove the corpse off the sidewalk into the gutter before he ran round the corner. By the time I got there he'd disappeared. Not a sign of him anywhere."

Detective–Sergeant Johnson of the Cape Town C.I.D. was the listener. He was temporarily in charge of the case by virtue of having been on duty at Caledon Square when the alarm was raised.

149

Now he was awaiting the arrival of his chief, Lieutenant Joubert.
He said: "And you're sure you'll recognise him again?"

"Never forget him. I saw him clearly. He had a mop of red hair
and a big nose, and a jutting lower lip. A young fellow. Yes, I'd
know him again."

By this time all necessary photographs had been taken, and Doc
McGregor had left with the body in the meat—wagon. Three uniformed policemen were dispersing the crowd. Most of them
reluctantly went their way, but several little groups had collected at
a safe distance and were still watching.

"All right, Bruyns," said Johnson. "You can go now, but you'll
have to come to Caledon Square in the morning to make a formal
statement. At any time before 10. Ask for Sergeant Coetzee. He'll
fix you up." He turned in a gesture of dismissal and spoke to one of
he policemen. "Lieutenant Joubert should be here in a couple of
minutes. Tell him I'm waiting for him in the lounge of the Britannia
Palace."

"Yessir," said the constable.

Johnson had barely reached a comfortable seat when Joubert
arrived. With him was Rolf le Roux, the inevitable pipe throwing a
smokescreen round his cheerful and bearded face. The three were
alone in the lounge.

They settled themselves while Johnson rapidly sketched what
had happened. "Nothing in his pockets," he said, "except some loose
change, a handkerchief and this wallet. Shall we go through it now?"

"Yes," said Joubert, and added: "Anybody in the crowd know who
he was?"

"No. Strangely, although I'm sure I'd never seen the guy before,
his face was somehow familiar. McGregor made a similar comment."
He was emptying the contents of the wallet onto the small table
around which they were sitting, and suddenly his face cleared. "Of
course," he said. He gestured to an envelope, pointing out the name
and address, "Edmund Mortimer. The actor. His picture was in the
Cape Mail this morning. He's the star of this English company
which is starting a Cape Town run at the Columbia next week."

Other letters and several visiting cards clinched the identification.

While Joubert and Johnson were going over these, Rolf picked up
and examined a folded newspaper clipping. He looked up, suddenly

interested. "These actors," he asked, "aren't they presenting a Shakespearian play?"

"Yes," said Johnson. "*Macbeth*. It was the sensation of their Johannesburg run. Why do you ask?"

"This clipping. Look, it is cut from the personal advertising column of the *Cape Planet*, tonight's issue, as you can see from the portion of the date above. Now read the advertisement that has been marked: 'The son of Duncan secretly lives in the English Court.' Duncan, if I remember correctly, is one of the characters in *Macbeth*. The taxi driver said Mortimer came out of this hotel, Britannia Palace — English Court. It seems to me this advertisement may be very relevant to the case."

"You mean, said Joubert, "that it's a coded invitation for Mortimer to come here?"

"Not necessarily Mortimer, but for someone to come here. Perhaps the night clerk could give us some information."

The clerk not only could, but was bubbling over with it. "Yes, I remember him perfectly. He came in and spoke to me. He wanted to know whether a lady was registered here, and when I told him she was, he asked if he could see her. But I noticed her key was on the hook here — as it still is — so she was obviously out. He seemed disappointed when I told him, but he wouldn't leave a note as I suggested. Just asked me to tell her an old friend had called."

"The name of the lady?" asked Joubert.

"Mrs. Albain."

Johnson straightened with inspiration. "Mrs. D. Albain?"

"Yes."

Joubert asked, in surprise: "Do you know her?"

"Not her," said Johnson. "Shakespeare. In *Macbeth*, Duncan had two sons — Malcolm and Donalbain. Donalbain — D. Albain. Association of ideas."

They looked at one another.

"Tell us everything you can about Mrs. Albain," said Joubert to the clerk. "I don't suppose you were here when she registered?"

"Luckily, I was. The regular day man had an attack of ap—pendicitis yesterday, and I was called in to help out. I attended to Mrs. Albain. Wait, here's the register. You can see from the entry she came in at 11.30 this morning. She paid for a week in advance. She had a small suitcase which was taken up to her room by the bell–hop."

"Yes, yes," said Joubert. "But what did she look like?"

"That's not easy to answer... She was wearing a hat which pretty well covered her hair, but what I could see of it was dark. Her face was heavily made up — but beautifully done, if you know what I mean. She was dressed very smartly, and she had a husky voice. Fairly tall for a woman, but everything else about her was in proportion. In her early thirties, I'd say. Brown eyes."

They digested this for a moment.

"Okay," said Joubert. "I think we'll have a look at Mrs. Albain's room. And you'd better come with us."

Like a funeral procession they filed in silence up the stairs and along the carpeted passage. At the door, the clerk knocked, waited a moment and then turned the key.

The only sign that the room had once been occupied was the suitcase next to the bed.

"I forgot to mention," said the clerk, "that a short while after registration I saw Mrs. Albain leaving the hotel."

"She won't be back," said Johnson. He had opened the suitcase, and now motioned to the contents. It was stuffed full of newspapers, torn and crumpled.

Joubert said: "All the same, I'm going to place a man in the lobby. If she does decide to return, there'll be someone to welcome her." He closed the suitcase and picked it up. "And I also think we'll take this to headquarters, and have the contents thoroughly sifted. Just in case."

They went to Caledon Square and for the next 15 minutes Joubert busied himself with routine. He gave the suitcase to Sergeant Botha; together with Johnson he prepared descriptions of the redheaded man and Mrs. Albain, and ordered a general alarm.

At the end of this time, Botha was back. "All old torn newspapers," he said, "with two exceptions. I've pasted the strips together for you with transparent tape. This one's complete, but parts of the other are still missing."

The completed strip of paper was a receipt from the *Cape Planet* for a personal advertisement for which cash had been paid. It was dated that day.

Joubert looked at the others significantly. "Seeing we found it in the suitcase, the time–table's pretty obvious, isn't it? She first put the notice in the paper, then went to the Britannia Palace to reserve the room.   I don't suppose there can be any doubt that the advertisement is the one marked by Mortimer.   Our missing lady seems to have been working very much in collaboration with the redheaded man."

"It's possible, but there are still objections, Dirk," said Rolf.   He shook his head slightly.

"Such as?"

"Well, if a trap was being laid to bring Mortimer to Britannia Palace, why was it necessary for the lady to show herself at all?   The advertisement would still have brought him there.   Why take any chance of being connected with the crime?

Joubert grinned suddenly. "You're not really asking questions, are you, old—timer?" he said. "Come on, what's on your mind?"

"There's a pattern running through this case that isn't normal. It seems simple on the surface, but there's still so much extra that has been added.   This woman registering at the hotel so un— necessarily is one example. The fact that the murderer returned to his victim to strike him again and roll his body into the gutter is another...   And the way he tailed him.   How did the taxi driver describe it, Johnson? Oh yes. 'Like a kid showing off.' "

"And what do you make of all that, Oom Rolf?"

"This, Dirk. The actions are exaggerated, in the same way as a performer on stage exaggerates over real life to make his point with the audience. And that is another recurring pattern: the murdered man was an actor. He was brought to the scene of his death by an advertisement which had a reference to a play. And this woman and the murderer? Weren't they also... theatrical?"

"So you think they were actors? That's more than possible."

"Not actors, Dirk. One actor. The pattern is too similar for it to be the work of more than one person. Someone who played two parts today — both the woman and the redheaded man — and someone who looks nothing like either in real life."

Johnson asked: "And you don't know whether the murderer is a man or a woman?" He did not wait for an answer. "You know there are indications that it is a woman. This advertisement... A secret meeting in an hotel is more likely to be between a man and a woman than between two men."

"That's not certain," said Joubert, and hesitated. He picked up the receiver of his telephone and asked to be connected with Doc McGregor. The call came after a short delay. "Listen, doc, I've got a query for you. Could the blows on the murdered man tonight have been struck by a woman?"

"Maybe yes," said McGregor, "and maybe no. They were verra fierce, those blows, but a lot will depend on the weight of the weapon. I'll tell you more when you find it, but in the meantime let a body ha' a bit of sleep. It seems every time I get into my pajamas — !"

Joubert replaced the receiver, his brow furrowed in thought. "If you're right, Oom... "

"I am right, Dirk. The murderer is an actor. Even so... "

"What?"

"It does not explain everything. Yes, I can understand acting to cover a motive and an identity, but the crime itself... Look, Dirk, the way Mortimer was struck down shows passion, great passion. I could have understood if he had been killed, and the murderer ran away. But this man came back, struck the victim again repeatedly, and rolled the body into the gutter. Acting, yes. But acting all the time over and above and through a violent personal emotion." Rolf's shoulders hunched in an involuntary shiver. "No, Dirk, we are still very far from the truth."

He shook his head and did not complete the next sentence: "The normal truth... "

Joubert turned his attention to the torn piece of pasteboard Botha had salvaged with the receipt. What it was, was obvious. It was a portion of a ticket issued by a railway station cloakroom for baggage deposited; but that section that showed the date and the station of issue was missing. He turned it over, and then his eyes gulped the portion of a sentence hand printed in heavy block letters.

Silently he put it on the desk in front of him, and his forefinger motioned the others to look.

The words read: BLOOD WILL HAVE BLOOD

ACT II

Six suspects. They sat in Joubert's office, with the morning sun streaming through the window. Six suspects, all excited, shocked and curious. And all acting.

The white–haired man with the upright carriage and very blue eyes was talking. "No, this is all the company who are in Cape Town at present. The others will join us early next week."

Joubert asked: "Exactly where are they at the moment, Mr. Benton? Together?"

"No. Mr. and Mrs. Brock — Mrs. Brock is listed as Desiree Coppard on the programme you have there, Inspector — and their daughter, Shirley, are on their way down by car. They're somewhere on the Garden Route now. Then there's Teale and Franklin — William Teale and Raymond Franklin — they're staying with some relatives of Teale's at... What's the name of that place again?"

His whole gesture of interrogation was an appeal to his audience to help him over his mental hiatus.

The gaunt woman with the sinister face said: "Beaufort West, Cyril."

Johnson refreshed his memory by glancing at the programme. Her name was Arlene Crispin, and she played the part of Second Witch. Johnson thought: "Type casting?" and gave a mental grin.

Benton was still talking. "Thank you, Arlene. Then there's Philip Dyke, Lieutenant. He flew from Johannesburg to Durban to attend to some business, and will take a plane down here in a day or so. And then there's Mrs. Farnsworth — acting name, Frances Cornier. Where is Frances now, Leo?"

Yes. There they were on the programme: Lady Macbeth — Frances Cornier; Macduff — Leo Farnsworth.

The bronzed man with the thinning hair and the mournful look said: "Still in the eastern Transvaal, I imagine. Tomorrow she should begin to make her way back to Johannesburg." He added, almost in a stage aside to the police officials: "She's been touring the Kruger Park with friends, the Ashburtons, in their caravan. I'm not quite sure where she is, at the moment."

"Thank you." There was an undertone of briskness in Joubert's voice. "Mr. Benton, you are the director of the company?"

The limelight shifted again to the white–haired man. "Yes," he said.

"I'd like you to remain here for a few minutes after the others have left... Now, you people, I want you to understand one thing clearly. You are free to go anywhere, do anything, as long as you don't attempt to leave town. For a while at least all of you will be

under surveillance. You are all suspects. Not one of you has so far
produced a provable alibi for the time of the murder, and we have to
take every precaution. I would like to add that I will be available on
request to have a private and confidential interview with anyone
who feels such a meeting could help solve this case. Thank you, and
good morning."

They released the attitudes they had struck, and made a
dignified exit. The room seemed strangely empty with only Joubert,
Johnson, Rolf le Roux and Cyril Benton.

The actor said: "I can understand the men being under suspicion,
but why the women? After all, Mortimer was killed by a man."

Johnson spoke: "Or by a woman disguised as a man."

"I see. Or by a man disguised as another man. Yes. And we are
a company of actors. Now it's obvious what you're thinking. False
face must hide what the false heart doth know. It's possible."

Rolf sat up with sudden interest.

"Tell me, Mr. Benton," he said. "That expression you used —
about a false face — isn't that a quotation from *Macbeth*?"

"Yes... Oh dear, I shouldn't have said it, of course."

"Shouldn't? Why not?"

"It's an old and rather powerful stage superstition. It's supposed
to bring disaster if you quote from that play, except in the normal
course of performance or rehearsal. One doesn't even mention the
title in public or private conversation. Most actors use 'the Scottish
play' or other pseudonyms."

Rolf said: "Interesting... Yet the words slipped very easily from
your tongue. Why, this time, did you forget the taboo?"

"Well, this situation is rather unprecedented and shocking, isn't
it? Enough to make anyone forget an old habit. Besides, we ended
a very successful run in Johannesburg with Scot, and are starting off
with it in Cape Town. The words are very much on the edge of my
consciousness."

"I see. Is this a normal reaction? Do you invariably quote lines
from the current play?"

"Not only me, Mr. le Roux — every actor. Our whole cast
continually interlard their conversation with quotations from the
Bard. It may seem a strange phenomenon to you, but among players
it's universal."

"And the lines you quote — are they always extracts from your own part?"

"Not necessarily, although naturally your own lines spring more readily to your lips than any others. I've stressed it may seem a strange habit to a layman, but there is a logical explanation."

"And that is?"

"Well, each time an actor plays a character, a portion of him becomes that character. A sort of self–identification. And I've noticed that when you quote anybody else's lines, they are generally those you'd have liked to have played yourself."

Joubert interrupted impatiently. "Yes, yes. Now, Mr. Benton, there are one or two questions I must ask you. First, I see from your programme you have nobody playing the part of Donalbain. Has that always been the case?"

"As far as this tour is concerned — yes. You see, Lieutenant, we're a small company. We've had to amend the script that Shakespeare wrote. Actually, three parts have been omitted — Donalbain, Lennox and Hecate. Several of us also double parts, as you can see. I play Duncan and the Old Man; Teal is Fleance, Young Siward and the English Doctor; Enid Cooke is Lady Macduff and the Nurse; Dyke handles both Banquo and Old Siward; Franklin is Ross and the Scottish Doctor; and Golden triples up as Seyton, the Sergeant and the Porter. We manage the few non–speaking parts by dressing–up stage hands and volunteer amateur actors."

While Benton was speaking, Johnson once again was sorting and correlating his impressions. Enid Cooke he had placed — she was the tiny brunette with the large eyes who was sitting near the door. And George Golden must have been the man next to her — the young fellow, very short and almost abnormally thick–set. That left the stoutish woman who had sat next to Farnsworth, and — yes — there was only one name unaccounted for on the cast list. Valerie Stribling. Playing the Third Witch.

Joubert was saying: "I see. And Mortimer, of course, was Mac–beth. What are you going to do now that he is dead? Cancel the play?"

"Certainly not. The show must go on, you know. Farnsworth has been understudying Mortimer, so he'll naturally take over the part. Fortunately, Duncan and Macduff never appear together, so I can easily take over Farnsworth's role. With cuts in a few minor speeches, we'll get by."

"I take it Farnsworth must have realised that if anything happened to Mortimer, he'd play the lead?"

"Certainly. But what... Oh come now, Lieutenant, if you're looking for motives, surely you can pick something better? Of course Farnsworth would like to play the part — but to murder for it? Rubbish!"

Joubert said: "I admit that's probably far–fetched, but you'll realise there must be a motive for the killing."

"Yes, but I think you hit the wrong angle this time. Actually, Farnsworth was the only member of the cast on good terms with Mortimer. He was much too temperamental — Mortimer, I mean — to really get on with anyone. I, for one, quarrelled with him several times. But I must admit he was popular with the ladies."

"I see. And who was the lady in your cast to whom he paid particular attention?"

"None of them," said Benton, and hesitated. "As a matter of fact, Lieutenant, I think that caused quite a bit of resentment among some of them — although I've no real proof of that. The point is that Mortimer obviously had some lady–love in Johannesburg. You see, it was quite well known that he was not — well, not of a celibate nature, and when he used to disappear after rehearsals and shows, it followed that tongues started wagging."

"And he never mentioned where he'd gone?"

"No, but I think I know all the same."

"Yes?"

"I saw him one afternoon — just by accident, of course — going into a small hotel in President Street. The Piccadilly, I think it was called. And then, a couple of times afterwards, I saw him in the same vicinity."

Joubert said: "I see. Well, I think that's all for the — "

It was Rolf's turn to interrupt: "No, Dirk. I still have a couple of questions, Mr. Benton. I'm very interested in the way an actor identifies with the part he plays, There are things in this case. Tell me, is there any action in *Macbeth* where a man is struck many times over the head, and his body pushed into the gutter?"

"Not struck, no. Stabbed. And not a gutter — a ditch."

"Yes?"

"When one of the murderers reports back to Macbeth after assassinating Banquo, he uses the words: Deep in a ditch he lies, with twenty trenched gashes in his head, the least a death to nature. Do you think that has any significance?"

"I do." Rolf was strangely excited. "Mr. Benton, I'd like to come with you now, and get a copy of the script you use in the play. It's possible clues to the solution of the murder can be found there."

"And I," said Joubert, with a wink to Johnson, will still put my trust in police routine. Good reading, Oom!"

ACT III

Memorandum from Detective–Sergeant van Zyl to Lieutenant Joubert. Subject: Out of town suspects.

The following movements of out of town suspects have been ascertained:

Philip Dyke staying at Majestic Hotel, Durban. Went out with friends last night, returning at approximately 10 p.m. Impossible for him by any means to have reached Cape Town in time for the murder.

William Teale and Raymond Franklin staying with Mr. and Mrs. R. C. Prentice at Beaufort West. Teale and Franklin left by car early yesterday, ostensibly to visit friends on farm near Graaff–Reinet. Possible for them to have reached Cape Town by midday. Only expected back at Beaufort West this evening. Farm they are supposed to be visiting not on telephone, but Graaff–Reinet police are sending man out to investigate. Report later.

Man, woman and young girl registered at Pinero Hotel in Oudtshoorn at 8 p.m. last night, in the name of Brock. Answer to description of suspects. Left early this morning for Knysna. Police there checking further.

No definite information about Frances Cornier (Mrs. Farnsworth) or Mr. and Mrs. Ashburton, in whose caravan she is supposed to be touring the Kruger Park. Ashburton let Johannesburg five days ago. Car bearing their registration number and pulling a caravan observed by Game Warden at Pretorius Kop yesterday. Police at Nelspruit and Pilgrim's Rest investigating.

Memorandum from Sergeant J. Coetzee to Lieutenant Joubert.

Subject: Investigations at theatre.

Acting on instructions and on information received that there
would be a meeting of performers at Midday today, I went thee at
11.30 a.m. together with the witness, Bruyns. We observed all the
performers arriving, but Bruyns was unable to positively identify
any one of them.

While the meeting was in progress, I interviewed Edgar
Correnda, who is the stage manager and in charge of the properties
of the touring company. He alleges that a red wig is missing from a
box of similar wigs (statement attached). The box was not secured,
and any member of the cast could have had access to the room where
it was kept.

Telex message from Lieutenant Mackenzie, Johannesburg, to
Lieutenant Joubert, Cape Town:

Reference query Piccadilly Hotel. Manager remembers Mortimer
calling several times to see woman registered as Mrs. D. Albain,
Latter did not use room for sleeping. Claimed she was a manu-
facturer's representative and wanted room as temporary office.
Mortimer's only known visitor. Albain's description: Tall, dark hair,
brown eyes, husky voice, stylish dresser. Any further queries?

Deep in the comfortable chair in his room, Rolf le Roux had
allowed his pipe to stay unlit for over five minutes.

He ran his fingers slowly through his beard, and in his
concentration stared at nothing – but behind that nothing was a
vapour in the image of a man. The image stalked something, and it's
movements were not quite stealthy. They gave subtle flounces, this
way and that, to... what? Attract attention? No, more than that. To
boast.

A braggart. Yes. And Mrs. Albain, of course. It fitted. The
quotation...

He added another line to the long list on the paper in front of
him: O I could play the woman with my eyes and braggart with my
tongue.

No, it didn't quite fit. That was Macduff's speech — his cry for
revenge. But the crime itself, the coming back to strike and strike

again, the twenty trenched gashes, that was Macbeth. And the red wig, the gory locks. They were Banquo's gory locks. No unity. No straight pattern.

Three into one won't go. Now, if it had been two into one... But it had to go. There had to be rhyme and reason. Cause and effect. Perhaps deeper down...

Again his eyes pushed through the nothingness. There was something... He caught it for a second, lost it, caught it again. Not with a flash of triumph; almost with a sense of epic tragedy. He brooded.

He stood up suddenly and walked across to the bookcase. On the top shelf was a manilla file, one of many, and inside were numerous newspaper clippings. The name on the cover was "John George Haigh."

He sat down again, his thoughts still dull and lowering. Almost automatically he struck a match, and held it to his pipe. Through the flame he read the first few words...

Memorandum from Detective–Sergeant Botha to Lieutenant Joubert.
Subject: Advertisement receipt and cloakroom ticket.

Dulcie Greenway, female clerk at *Cape Planet*, remembers receiving advertisement and issuing receipt. States it was paid for in cash by tall dark woman. Would recognise her again.

Am experiencing difficulty with cloakroom ticket. Absence of date and station of issue makes task almost impossible. Railway police suggest investigation be deferred until further details are available. Thousands of items annually are unclaimed from cloak–rooms all over the country.

Urgent telephoned report from Detective–Sergeant van Zyl to Lieutenant Joubert:

A telex message has just been received from Graaff–Reinet confirming that Teale and Franklin have an alibi for the time of the murder. No news yet from police at George or the eastern Transvaal.

Midday reports from operatives shadowing suspects show men

have kept together all morning. Women separated, but none did anything suspicious after leaving your office. Entire cast at the moment are attending a meeting on the stage of the Columbia Theatre.

Detective–Constable Barends, on duty at Columbia Theatre, reports the discovery of a parcel of women's clothing wedged between the wall and a drainpipe within reach of a window of one of he dressing–rooms. A maid on the premises has identified the dress as belonging to Miss Arlene Crispin. Rushed the clothing to the Britannia Palace Hotel, where the clerk has identified the dress as the one worn by Mrs. Albain. Have instructed Barends to bring Crispin to you immediately for questioning.

After he put the file down, Rolf moved with a new purpose. He took up his pen and a clean sheet of paper. He drew a line lengthwise down the centre of the paper, and then put headings at the top of each column. On the left he wrote 'Victims' and on the right 'Avengers'. Then, in each column he began to transcribe quotations from his original list.

When he finished, he stared at the document for a long time, because he wanted to be wrong. But he could find no flaw. The pattern was plain. Perfect. Horribly unshakeable.

His thoughts twisted.

Guilt. A terrible motive, driving to destruction. Blood will have blood... All the perfumes... If only it was normal.

He reached for the telephone.

ACT IV

The tall woman with the sinister face would not be browbeaten. "You can take up any attitude you like," she said, "but I've told you the truth. The clothes are mine, but I hadn't noticed they were gone from my wardrobe. Not for several days, anyway. I didn't hide them behind the drainpipe — why should I? As far as access to them is concerned, my dressing–room door is always open, and so is the closet where I keep my clothes."

Joubert was rattled, but he concealed this by accenting a strong tone of doubt. "Is that so?" he said. "And I suppose you will also tell me you had no motive for killing Edmund Mortimer?"

This rank shot in the dark somehow reached a target. The woman paled, said defiantly: "A motive doesn't prove I did anything."

"No? Look, Miss Crispin, you're in a very serious position. Just how serious I don't think you realise. I'm going to postpone this interview for an hour. By then I hope you'll have decided to tell the truth."

A uniformed man led her away as the telephone rang.

Rolf.

"Hullo, Oom," said Joubert, "You're missing all the excitement. We've got our main suspect here in a cell. I expect she'll confess shortly."

"A woman? No, Dirk, you're wrong. I know everything about this case... "

"Everything? I'm prepared to bet we know far more than you do. We're only short of one or two points. Nothing now needs explanation except where the cloakroom ticket was issued, and just what was deposited there."

"I can tell you both things," said Rolf, and there was urgency in his voice. "The cloakroom is almost certainly at Johannesburg station, and what was deposited there is a trunk — a fairly large trunk because it contains a body."

Joubert said, almost stupidly: "A body?"

"Yes, the body of the woman who called herself Mrs. Albain."

"Another murder?"

"No, suicide. Listen, Dirk, we've no time to lose — and that's why I don't want to explain now. Believe me, I know the pattern of this murder, and it's not complete. We must get these actors together before more lives are lost. Immediately!"

"At this moment they're all at the Columbia Theatre."

"Then that's where we must go. I'll meet you there, Hurry!"

Joubert shook his head as though to clear it, made a movement to leave his chair, and then changed his mind. He picked up the telephone again, spoke to the switchboard operator, and then waited impatiently while she got his number and asked for the man to whom he wished to speak. A voice came over the wire.

Joubert barked: "Barends? Lieutenant Joubert. How many of our men are in or near the theatre? Five? Good. Now look. I want a man stationed at every possible exit. And you'd better warn the acting company — in fact, everyone in the theatre — not to try and leave until I get down there. Right. Hop to it."

Only then did he go down the stairs into the street and start threading his little Austin through the traffic.

He arrived at the theatre just as Rolf was paying off his taxi. Barends greeted both of them.

"Your orders have been carried out, sir," he told Joubert. "All exits are covered and I've warned the performers and stage hands to stay put."

Rolf said: "You warned? Oh no!" He almost ran into the theatre.

The cast were there, waiting on–stage under a blaze of lights, and Benton stepped forward to greet them. He spoke with petulance. "What's this all about, Lieutenant? I realise you have your duty to do, but the cast has already been badly upset — "

Rolf interrupted, almost fiercely: "Farnsworth? Where's Farnsworth?"

"He's down there — no, he isn't... Has anyone seen Leo?"

"He was in the wings a few minutes ago," said a stage hand. "He was walking towards those stairs."

Rolf said: "Quick! It might not be too late!" He ran, followed by Joubert and Benton. Other members of the cast straggled behind.

The stairs were iron and a narrow spiral. They led to the roof. The oak door at the top was open.

The ladder was lying where it had been kicked at the foot of the flagpole. Instead of a flag there was a body at the top of the mast, gripped by a rope around the throat and still swaying slightly. They knew it was Farnsworth despite the thick smears of greasepaint disfiguring his face, the artificial nose dangling from his left cheek, the fiery red wig halfway over one ear.

Benton gasped in shock. "How? ... Why? ..."

"Remember the last Act," said Rolf. "The scene where Macbeth is at first unwilling to fight, and Macduff says— "

"Yes." Benton swallowed audibly. He began to quote:
"We'll have thee as our rarer monsters are
Painted upon a pole; and underwrit
'Here you may see the tyrant...'

❂

"The play," said Rolf, "is over."

EPILOGUE

The sun was already setting when Joubert, Rolf le Roux, Johnson and Benton, the theatrical company's director, all back in the Lieutenant's office, tucked into a delayed meal of sandwiches and coffee.

Before they had even settled down the telex reply to the urgent message to Johannesburg sent earlier that afternoon, was received. Joubert passed it around. It read: "Suspicions correct. Large trunk unclaimed at station contains body of woman. Cause of death, loss of blood, due to veins in wrist being severed. No other marks on body, and wounds appear to be self–inflicted. Have made preliminary identification of body from photograph of Frances Cornier (Mrs. Farnsworth). Full report later."

Rolf said: "I should have thought of that — I mean the cutting of the veins."

"I must admit," said Joubert, "that I don't know how you thought of anything. Personally, I'm still groping for an explanation. Was Farnsworth mad?"

"In the legal sense, no. He knew what he was doing, that it was wrong, and what the consequences of his actions would be. And yet he could no more have stopped himself doing what he did than you could stop your leg jerking if I tapped you below the knee–cap. That was the crux of the whole problem. As soon as I realised that the murderer must be a pure paranoiac, like the British multi–killer Haigh, the pattern started to take shape. Even so, I should have guessed it sooner. The actions were so purposive and yet so abnor-mal."

Benton shivered. "I thought I knew Leo Farnsworth, Mr. Le Roux. Tell me — what actually happened?"

"It's not a pretty story," said Rolf. "Just before he was due to leave Johannesburg, he discovered his wife had hired a room in the Piccadilly Hotel under the name of Mrs. Albain and was meeting a man there. He didn't know who the man was, but suspected he was a member of the cast. He taxed his wife with her unfaithfulness. Her reply was to take her own life.

"When Farnsworth found her body, he was obsessed with desire for revenge. He conceived a plan to find out the name of her lover. In order for it to be effective, he had to conceal the fact of her death. He telephoned the Ashburtons and told them his wife had been called away and so could not accompany them on their caravan trip. Then he hid the body in a trunk and deposited it in the cloakroom at Johannesburg station.

"Here in Cape Town, he put his plan into effect. Disguised as a woman, he inserted an advertisement in the *Cape Planet*, knowing that the cryptic phrase he used would lure the unknown lover to the Britannia Court Hotel. He registered there as Mrs. Albain, because he wanted the man to make an inquiry and then leave without being on his guard. The plan worked — Mortimer came and Farnsworth killed him. Then, later, when the woman whose clothes he had used for the Albain disguise was detained for questioning and when a further warning was given that nobody could leave the theatre until the police arrived, he felt the trap closing in and suicide was his only means of escape."

Rolf took four contemplative puffs of his pipe. "That's the story Farnsworth would have told had he lived. He'd even have believed it himself. On that evidence he would have been hanged. And the tragedy is it's not the true story."

Joubert asked: "What do you mean?"

"It's not true, Dirk, because it doesn't fully describe the facts. There is much more over and above the obvious story. So much more... the explanation of why the crime was committed the way it was."

"Some sort of mental kink?" hazarded Johnson.

"Yes. The twist in his mind which made him do what he did in the way that he did. In the way he couldn't help doing... You put me on the right track, Mr. Benton."

The actor was surprised. "I did?"

"Yes. Remember our conversation about actors identifying themselves with characters and speeches in plays? It was clear from the facts that somehow this real drama was closely tied in with the play *Macbeth*. The use of the name 'Mrs. D. Albain' for instance; the quotation written on the back of the cloakroom ticket; the very way in which the crime was committed — all the little things that were unnecessary and therefore abnormal. That's why I took the script from you, to see if I could trace other references, and so get an impression of the personality of the murderer. At this stage it was obvious that he or she had to be someone closely connected with the production."

"And you found?"

"Many things. Almost every aberration could be correlated with a speech in *Macbeth*. But the actual happenings were not exact duplications of actions or speeches in the play. It seemed the murderer took words and scenes from Shakespeare, not as they were, but as symbols of parallel emotions."

Johnson asked: "Was that the mental kink?"

"No. An absolutely normal person could react to circumstances in exactly the same way. What worried me, there seemed no coherent pattern of thought in the murder... Look at it this way. One would expect a sane man, an actor, to identify himself with the single character in the play. Perhaps even two characters if there was emotional conflict. But this murderer identified with three...

"Firstly, with the leading character. In the play Macbeth hires two murderers to kill Banquo — but when the deed is about to be done, a third murderer appears. Banquo is brutally killed and his body left in a ditch. In the real homicide, the compulsion was so strong, the killer took a big risk by returning to strike again and roll the body into the gutter... The point I am making is that, in the play the implication is that the third murderer is Macbeth in disguise, so the identification of the real killer with the role of Macbeth becomes quite clear.

"And there are numerous other indications. The quotation on the cloakroom ticket, for example — these words are spoken by and can only refer to Macbeth."

Benton said: "And the other character identifications?"

"They were very clear. Remember, Mortimer's murderer first disguised himself as a woman; then, when he put on the false nose and the wig, his actions were very peculiar. A witness described them as 'like a kid showing off.' In other words, like a boaster. There is a quotation in the play that fits the situation like a glove: 'O I could play the woman with my eyes, and braggart with my tongue.' The speaker was Macduff, and the rest of his speech is also significant. He goes on: 'But, gentle heavens, cut short all inter—mission; front to front bring thou this fiend of Scotland and myself; within my sword—length set him — if he escape — heaven forgive him too.' It's a cry for revenge — for revenge against Macbeth. That was the first paradox.

"The second was the red wig worn by the murderer. The reference in the play is to the scene where Banquo's ghost appears, and Macbeth calls out to it: 'Thou canst not say I did it... Never shake thy gory locks at me!' True, the speech is Macbeth's, but the 'gory locks' are so much a part of Banquo that the identification had to lie there. And that was when I became confused."

"I'm not surprised," said Joubert.

"Yes, there didn't appear to be any consistent pattern — even though, by that time, I knew what I had to find. You see, I'd already proved to my own satisfaction that Farnsworth was the murderer. He played Macduff and understudied Macbeth and, in a normal mental conflict I could easily see how he might identify with both characters.

"But I could visualise no reason for his identification with Banquo, until I realised that between him and Macduff there was indeed an affinity. Both had been cruelly wronged by Macbeth. And the type of mind in which one character can become the psychological equivalent of two other entirely different characters isn't a normal mind — it's the mind of a paranoiac, like John George Haigh.

"Once I reached this conclusion, the pieces fell into place. I realised that for a pattern to start, Mrs. Farnsworth must be dead. Violently dead. That would be the only possible cause of the new, strange position she was now occupying in her husband's mind. She'd become Lady Macbeth — the part she played on stage — and also the wife of the man who identified himself with Macduff. Her actual death was the spark, the initial shock that threw Farnsworth into a turmoil and brought about this tragedy.

"Look at it through his eyes: Lady Macduff was dead and, as in the play, Macbeth — that part of him that was Macbeth — was responsible for her demise. And on the other side, his real wife — Lady Macbeth in the play — was also dead. She ceased to live because of remorse at the deeds on her conscience. So, in a way, by his fearsome action on the streets of Cape Town, Macduff was avenging her, too... "

Joubert said slowly: "How did you know Mrs. Farnsworth had taken her own life?"

"Because Lady Macbeth committed suicide. The 'fiend–like

queen with self and violent hands'... Don't you see? It had to be that way. Or else the pattern would have been different. Farnsworth — the normal Farnsworth — must somehow have blamed himself for her unfaithfulness. Perhaps, to start with, it was no more than a regret that he'd neglected her — but the feeling had to be there to twist itself into a raging desire for revenge after her suicide.

"Revenge on those to blame. On her lover, yes — but on himself, too, because of his awful consciousness of personal guilt. Remember the oath he swore, the words written on the back of the cloakroom ticket? 'Blood will have blood.' Literally the blood of his wife which had pulsed from her cut veins because of himself, her lover and her own tortures of conscience... 'All the perfumes of Arabia will not sweeten this little hand'... "

Rolf shivered. "Horrible," he said, and then: "That is when the real Farnsworth ceased to exist. His mind twisted and distorted into a new entity Macbeth–Macduff–Banquo. A killer–avenger–victim... A warped and savage mind using his real dulled body only as a temporary disguise. And imagine the further shock that came to him when he realised his wife's lover was his own friend who acted Macbeth in the play... "

He stopped, and it was Johnson who broke the silence. "You've told us that fairly early in the case you deduced Farnsworth was the killer. How?"

Rolf smiled, "The advertisement, the deliberate decoying of the victim to a selected spot — an obvious ambush — all indicated a crime of revenge... When you, Mr. Benton told us Mortimer had been meeting someone clandestinely in Johannesburg, two points became clear to me. First, the person he met was probably a woman — someone known to his associates, but whose identity had to be concealed. And from that point, I realised the woman in all likelihood was married. The wife of an associate? What else could fit the circumstances?

"Then there was the word 'secretly' in the advertisement. It was unnecessarily inserted — the actual quotation reads: 'The son of Duncan lives in the English Court.' And that extra word indicated to me that the woman was supposed to be away from Cape Town at the time, although her husband was here. And, in the nature of things, that husband was the logical suspect.

"There were only two married couples in the cast — the Brocks and the Farnsworths. Mr. and Mrs. Brock were together with their daughter touring the Garden Route. No, it had to be Farnsworth."

Joubert asked: "So what was the hurry when you telephoned me this afternoon? With your information, we could first have found the trunk, and not thrown anyone into a panic. Or even without the trunk, once we'd traced the couple with whom Mrs. Farnsworth was supposed to be travelling, we would have guessed the rest. We could have moved quietly and methodically, and taken Farnsworth before he realised he was threatened."

"No, Dirk, there was danger. It's likely others would have died. You see, the pattern was incomplete. In the play, Macbeth killed many people, and perhaps what happened was all for the best. The pattern worked out quickly this way, just because of the threat to Farnsworth. Macbeth yielded to Macduff — and so was 'painted upon a pole' — and the criminal hanged."

"All the same," said Joubert, "I wish I'd have taken him alive."

"Do you?" Rolf leaned forward, gripping his pipe with both hands. "Do you really, Dirk? And what would have happened then? You'd have had him in the dock, with all the tortures of a trial, and he'd have told his story, and been hanged. As he was hanged, anyway. The difference would've been only the trial — and that would be a mockery.

"The courts aren't concerned with ultimate truth, only with evidence. So Farnsworth would be sentenced to death, because the law requires a capital sentence. He'd have been executed, not on his own responsibility, but on yours.

"And Dirk, knowing all the facts, would you still be prepared to declare that the tortured mind in his body really was Farnsworth?"

SOURCES

"The Newtonian Egg" first appeared in *Ellery Queen's Mystery Magazine*, December 1951.

"The Fifth Dimension" first appeared in *Ellery Queen's Mystery Magazine*, November 1952.

"Kill and Tell" first appeared in *Ellery Queen's Mystery Magazine*, December 1951.

"And Turn the Hour" first appeared in *Ellery Queen's Mystery Magazine*, September 1952.

"The Angel of Death" first appeared in *Spotlight*, Cape Town.

"Time Out of Mind" first appeared in *Milady*, Cape Town, 1948; *Ellery Queen's Mystery Magazine*, March, 1949.

"The Face of the Sphinx" first appeared in *Spotlight*, Cape Town.

"Little Fat Man" first appeared in *Ellery Queen's Prime Crimes 4*, ed. Eleanor Sullivan, 1986.

"The Flung–back Lid" first appeared in *John Creasey's Crime Collection*, 1979, ed. Herbert Harris.

"The Perfumes of Arabia" first appeared in *The Outspan*, South Africa.

THE NEWTONIAN EGG and other stories

✪

THE NEWTONIAN EGG and other stories by Peter Godfrey is set in 11–point Century font and printed on 60 pound natural shade opaque acid–free paper. The cover painting and the design are by Deborah Miller. The first edition comprises 200 copies in trade paper and 175 copies in cloth. THE NEWTONIAN EGG was published in February 2002 by Crippen & Landru, Publishers, Norfolk, Virginia.

Printed in the United States
4872

9 781885 941695